"*The depth, humanity and craft of this novel are as rich as the situation is stark.*" —SAMUEL R. DELANY

"*The yarn is a cluster of alien worlds evolving against the background of Paradise: the harshly physical one of Alyx, the overly simplified deterministic one of Machine, the wishful-thinking, artificial one of Gunnar. The most fascinating thing is watching the picnickers choose what parts of the world around them they want to believe; some learning to accept more of it as it's hammered home to them, some learning to duck the more intolerable realities more efficiently than before; the whole thing presented so convincingly that I really thought Miss Russ was going to kill off her heroine. In fact, I'm still not quite sure she didn't. . . .*" —HAL CLEMENT

JOANNA RUSS was born in 1937. She writes: "I spent my childhood half in the Bronx Zoo and half in the Botanical Gardens. I remember being enchanted with dinosaurs, mammoths, the Planetarium, all sorts of wild empty lots around my house (the Bronx was wilder then). I was one of the top ten Westinghouse Science Talent Search Winners in my last year in high school . . . I decided that I would rather go on with poetry. People told me: why don't you become a science fiction writer? I just laughed."

Joanna Russ's short stories have appeared frequently in the major science fiction magazines, as well as in literary magazines, and a number of her short plays have been performed, with good notices. Her first novel, PICNIC ON PARADISE, was published in 1968 as an Ace Science Fiction Special and was a nominee for the Nebula Award as best sf novel of the year. AND CHAOS DIED is her second novel.

PICNIC ON PARADISE

JOANNA RUSS

ace books
A Division of Charter Communications Inc.
1120 Avenue of the Americas
New York, N.Y. 10036

PICNIC ON PARADISE

Printed in U.S.A.

S HE WAS A SOFT-SPOKEN, DARK-HAIRED, SMALL-boned woman, not even coming up to their shoulders, like a kind of dwarf or miniature—but that was normal enough for a Mediterranean Greek of nearly four millennia ago, before super-diets and hybridization from seventy colonized planets had turned all humanity (so she had been told) into Scandinavian giants. The young lieutenant, who was two meters and a third tall, or three heads more than herself, very handsome and ebony-skinned, said "I'm sorry, ma'am, but I cannot believe you're the proper Trans-Temporal Agent; I think —" and he finished his thought on the floor, his head under one of his ankles and this slight young woman (or was she young? Trans-Temp did such strange things sometimes!) somehow holding him down in a position he could not get out of without hurting himself to excruciation. She let him go. She sat down on the balloon-inflated thing they provided for sitting on in these strange times, looking curiously at the super-men and

5

super-women, and said, "I am the Agent. My name is Alyx," and smiled. She was in a rather good humor. It still amused her to watch this whole place, the transparent columns the women wore instead of clothing, the parts of the walls that pulsated in and out and changed color, the strange floor that waved like grass, the three-dimensional vortices that kept springing to life on what would have been the ceiling if it had only stayed in one place (but it never did) and the general air of unhappy, dogged, insistent, sad restlessness. "A little bit of home," the lieutenant had called it. He had seemed to find particular cause for nostalgia in a lime-green coil that sprang out of the floor whenever anybody dropped anything, to eat it up, but it was "not in proper order" and sometimes you had to fight it for something you wanted to keep. The people moved her a little closer to laughter. One of them leaned toward her now.

"Pardon me," said this one effusively—it was one of the ladies—"but is that face yours? I've heard Trans-Temp does all sorts of cosmetic work and I thought they might—"

"Why yes," said Alyx, hoping against hope to be impolite. "Are those breasts yours? I can't help noticing—"

"Not at all!" cried the lady happily. "Aren't they wonderful? They're Adrian's. I mean they're by Adrian."

"I think that's enough," said the lieutenant.

"Only we *rather wondered*," said the lady, elevating her indigo brows at what she seemed to have taken as an insult, "why you keep yourself so covered up. Is it a tribal rite? Are you deformed? Why don't you get

6

cosmetic treatment; you could have asked for it, you know, I mean I think you could—" but here everybody went pale and turned aside, just as if she had finally managed to do something offensive and *All I did,* she thought, *was take off my shift.*

One of the nuns fell to praying.

"All right, Agent," said the lieutenant, his voice a bare whisper, "we believe you. Please put on your clothes.

"Please, Agent," he said again, as if his voice were failing him, but she did not move, only sat naked and cross-legged with the old scars on her ribs and belly showing in a perfectly natural and expectable way, sat and looked at them one by one: the two nuns, the lady, the young girl with her mouth hanging open and the iridescent beads wound through three feet of hair, the bald-headed boy with some contraption strapped down over his ears, eyes and nose, the artist and the middle-aged political man, whose right cheek had begun to jump. The artist was leaning forward with his hand cupped under one eye in the old-fashioned and nearly unbelievable pose of someone who has just misplaced a contact lens. He blinked and looked up at her through a flood of mechanical tears.

"The lieutenant," he said, coughing a little, "is thinking of anaesthetics and the lady of surgery—I really think you had better put your clothes back on, by the way—and as to what the others think I'm not so sure. I myself have only had my usual trouble with these damned things and I don't really mind—"

"Please, Agent," said the young officer.

"But I don't think," said the artist, massaging one eye, "that you quite understand the effect you're creating."

"None of *you* has anything on," said Alyx.

"You have on your history," said the artist, "and we're not used to that, believe me. Not to history. Not to old she-wolves with livid marks running up their ribs and arms, and not to the idea of fights in which people are neither painlessly killed nor painlessly fixed up but linger on and die—slowly—or heal—slowly.

"Well!" he added, in a very curious tone of voice, "after all, we may all look like that before this is over."

"Buddha, no!" gasped a nun.

Alyx put her clothes on, tying the black belt around the black dress. "You may not look as bad," she said a bit sourly. "But you will certainly smell worse.

"And I," she added conversationally, "don't like pieces of plastic in people's teeth. I think it disgusting."

"Refined sugar," said the officer. "One of our minor vices," and then, with an amazed expression, he burst into tears.

"Well, well," muttered the young girl, "we'd better get on with it."

"Yes," said the middle-aged man, laughing nervously, " 'People for Every Need,' you know," and before he could be thoroughly rebuked for quoting the blazon of the Trans-Temporal Military Authority (Alyx heard the older woman begin lecturing him on the nastiness of calling anyone even by insinuation a thing, an agency, a means or an instrument, *anything* but a People, or as she said "a People People") he began to lead the file toward the door, with the girl coming next, a green tube in the middle of her mouth, the two nuns clinging together in shock, the bald-headed boy swaying a little as he walked, as if to unheard music, the lieutenant and the artist—who lingered.

"Where'd they pick you up?" he said, blinking again and fingering one eye.

"Off Tyre," said Alyx. "Where'd they pick *you* up?"

"We," said the artist, "are rich tourists. Can you believe it? Or refugees, rather. Caught up in a local war. A war on the surface of a planet, mind you; I don't believe I've heard of that in my lifetime."

"I have," said Alyx, "quite a few times," and with the lightest of light pushes she guided him toward the thing that passed for a decent door, the kind of thing she had run through, roaring with laughter, time after time at her first day at Trans-Temp, just for the pleasure of seeing it open up like a giant mouth and then pucker shut in an enormous expression of disgust.

"Babies!" she said.

"By the way," called back the artist, "I'm a flat-color man. What was your profession?"

"Murderer," said Alyx, and she stepped through the door.

"Raydos is the flat-color man," said the lieutenant, his feet up on what looked gratifyingly like a table. "Used to do wraparounds and walk-ins—very good walk-ins, too, I have a little education in that line myself—but he's gone wild about something called pigment on flats. Says the other stuff's too easy."

"Flats whats?" said Alyx.

"I don't know, any flat surface, I suppose," said the lieutenant. "And he's got those machines in his eyes which keep coming out, but he won't get retinotherapy. Says he likes having two kinds of vision. Most of us are born myopic nowadays, you know."

"I wasn't," said Alyx.

"Iris," the lieutenant went on, palming something and then holding it to his ear, "is pretty typical, though: young, pretty stable, ditto the older woman—oh yes, her name's Maudey—and Gavrily's a conamon, of course."

"Conamon?" said Alyx, with some difficulty.

"Influence," said the lieutenant, his face darkening a little. "Influence, you know. I don't like the man. That's too personal an evaluation, of course, but damn it, I'm a decent man. If I don't like him, I say I don't like him. He'd honor me for it."

"Wouldn't he kick your teeth in?" said Alyx.

"How much did they teach you at Trans-Temp?" said the lieutenant, after a pause.

"Not much," said Alyx.

"Well, anyway," said the lieutenant, a little desperately, "you've got Gavrily and he's a conamon, then Maudey—the one with the blue eyebrows, you know—"

"Dyed?" asked Alyx politely.

10

"Of course. Permanently. And the wienie—"

"Well, well!" said Alyx.

"You know," said the lieutenant, with sarcastic restraint, "you can't drink that stuff like wine. It's distilled. Do you know what distilled means?"

"Yes," said Alyx. "I found out the hard way."

"All right," said the lieutenant, jumping to his feet, "all right! A wienie is a wienie. He's the one with the bald head. He calls himself Machine because he's an idiotic adolescent rebel and he wears that—that Trivia on his head to give himself twenty-four hours a day of solid nirvana, station NOTHING, turns off all stimuli when you want it to, operates psionically. We call it a Trivia because that's what it is and because forty years ago it was a Tri-V and I *despise* bald young inexistential rebels who refuse to relate!"

"Well, well," she said again.

"And the nuns," he said, "are nuns, whatever that means to you. It means nothing to me; I am not a religious man. You have got to get them from here to there, 'across the border' as they used to say, because they had money and they came to see Paradise and Paradise turned into—" He stopped and turned to her.

"You know all this," he said accusingly.

She shook her head.

"Trans-Temp—"

"Told me nothing."

"Well," said the lieutenant, "perhaps it's best. Perhaps it's best. What we need is a person who knows nothing. Perhaps that's exactly what we need."

"Shall I go home?" said Alyx.

"Wait," he said harshly, "and don't joke with me. Paradise is the world you're on. It's in the middle of a commercial war. I said commercial war; I'm military and I have nothing to do here except get killed trying to make sure the civilians are out of the way. That's what you're for. You get them" (he pressed something in the wall and it turned into a map; she recognized it instantly, even though there were no sea-monsters and no four winds puffing at the corners, which was rather a loss) "from here to here," he said. "B is a neutral base. They can get you off-planet."

"Is that all?"

"No, that's not all. Listen to me. If you want to exterminate a world, you blanket it with hell-bombs and for the next few weeks you've got a beautiful incandescent disk in the sky, very ornamental and very dead, and that's that. And if you want to strip-mine, you use something a little less deadly and four weeks later you go down in heavy shielding and dig up any damn thing you like, and *that's* that. And if you want to colonize, we have something that kills every form of animal and plant life on the planet and then you go down and cart off the local flora and fauna if they're poisonous or use them as mulch if they're usable. But you can't do any of that on Paradise."

She took another drink. She was not drunk.

"There is," he said, "every reason not to exterminate Paradise. There is every reason to keep her just as she

12

is. The air and the gravity are near perfect, but you can't farm Paradise."

"Why not?" said Alyx.

"Why not?" said he. "Because it's all up and down and nothing, that's why. It's glaciers and mountains and coral reefs; it's rainbows of inedible fish in continental slopes; it's deserts, cacti, waterfalls going nowhere, rivers that end in lakes of mud and skies—and sunsets—and that's all it is. That's *all*." He sat down.

"Paradise," he said, "is impossible to colonize, but it's still too valuable to mess up. It's too beautiful." He took a deep breath. "It happens," he said, "to be a tourist resort."

Alyx began to giggle. She put her hand in front of her mouth but only giggled the more; then she let go and hoorawed, snorting derisively, bellowing, weeping with laughter.

"That," said the lieutenant stiffly, "is pretty ghastly." She said she was sorry.

"I don't know," he said, rising formally, "just what they are going to fight this war with. Sound on the buildings, probably; they're not worth much; and for the people every nasty form of explosive or neuronic hand-weapon that's ever been devised. But no radiation. No viruses. No heat. Nothing to mess up the landscape or the ecological balance. Only they've got a net stretched around the planet that monitors everything up and down the electromagnetic spectrum. Automatically, each millisecond. If you went out in those mountains, young woman, and merely sharpened your knife on a rock, the sparks

13

would bring a radio homer in on you in fifteen seconds. No, less."

"Thank you for telling me," said she, elevating her eyebrows.

"No fires," he said, "no weapons, no transporation, no automatic heating, no food processing, nothing airborne. They'll have some infra red from you but they'll probably think you're local wildlife. But by the way, if you hear anything or see anything overhead, we think the best thing for all of you would be to get down on all fours and pretend to be yaks. I'm not fooling."

"Poseidon!" said she, under her breath.

"Oh, one other thing," he said. "We can't have induction currents, you know. Might happen. You'll have to give up everything metal. The knife, please."

She handed it over, thinking *If I don't get that back—*

"Trans-Temp sent a synthetic substitute, of course," the lieutenant went on briskly. "And crossbows—same stuff—and packs, and we'll give you all the irradiated food we can get you. And insulated suits."

"And ignorance," said she. His eyebrows went up.

"Sheer ignorance," she repeated. "The most valuable commodity of all. Me. No familiarity with mechanical transportation or the whatchamacallits. Stupid. Can't read. Used to walking. Never used a compass in my life. Right?"

"Your skill—" he began.

From each of her low sandals she drew out what had looked like part of the ornamentation and flipped both knives expertly at the map on the wall—both

14

hands, simultaneously—striking precisely at point A and point B.

"You can have those, too," she said.

The lieutenant bowed. He pressed the wall again. The knives hung in a cloudy swirl, then in nothing, clear as air, while outside appeared the frosty blue sky, the snowy foothills drawing up to the long, easy swelling crests of Paradise's oldest mountain chain—old and easy, not like some of the others, and most unluckily, only two thousand meters high.

"By God!" said Alyx, fascinated, "I don't believe I've ever seen snow before."

There was a sound behind her, and she turned. The lieutenant had fainted.

They weren't right. She had palmed them a hundred times, flipped them, tested their balance, and they weren't right. Her aim was off. They felt soapy. She complained to the lieutenant, who said you couldn't expect exactly the same densities in synthetics, and sat shivering in her insulated suit in the shed, nodding now and again at the workers assembling their packs, while the lieutenant appeared and disappeared into the walls, a little frantically. "Those are just androids," said Iris good-humoredly. "Don't nod to them. Don't you think it's *fun*?"

"Go cut your hair," said Alyx.

Iris's eyes widened.

"And tell that other woman to do the same," Alyx added.

"Zap!" said Iris cryptically, and ambled off. It was detestably chilly. The crossbows impressed her, but she had had no time to practice with them (*Which will be remedied by every one of you bastards,* she thought) and no time to get used to the cold, which all the rest of them seemed to like. She felt stupid. She began to wonder about something and tried to catch the lieutenant by the arm, cursing herself in her own language, trying to think in her own language and failing, giving up on the knives and finally herding everyone outside into the snow to practice with the crossbows. The wienie was surprisingly good. He stayed at it two hours after the others drifted off, repeating and repeating; Iris came back with her cut hair hanging around her face and confided that she had been named after part of a camera; the lieutenant's hands began to shake a little on each appearance; and Machine became a dead shot. She stared at him. All the time he had kept the thing he wore on his head clamped over ears and eyes and nose. "He can see through it if he wants to," said Iris. Maudey was talking earnestly in a corner with Gavrily, the middle-aged politician, and the whole thing was taking on the air of a picnic. Alyx grew exasperated. She pinched a nerve in the lieutenant's arm the next time he darted across the shed and stopped him, he going "aaah!" and rubbing his arm; he said, "I'm very sorry, but—" She did it again.

"Look here," she said, "I may be stupid, but I'm not that stupid—"

"Sorry," he said, and was gone again, into one of the walls, right into one of the walls.

"He's busy," said Raydos, the flat-color man. "They're sending someone else through and he's trying to talk them out of it."

"Joy," said Alyx.

"Have you noticed," said Raydos, "how your vocabulary keeps expanding? That's the effect of hypnotic language training; they can't give you the whole context consciously, you see, only the sectors where the languages overlap so you keep coming up against these unconscious, 'buried' areas where a sudden context triggers off a whole pre-implanted pattern. It's like packing your frazzle; you always remember where it is when you need it, but of course it's always at the bottom. You'll be feeling rather stupid for a few days, but it'll wear off."

"A frazzle?" said Maudey, drifting over. "Why, I imagine she doesn't even know what a frazzle is."

"I told you to cut your hair," said Alyx.

"A frazzle," said Gavrily, "is the greatest invention of the last two centuries, let me assure you. Only in some cities, of course; they have a decibel limit on most. And of course it's frazzles, one for each ear; they neutralize the sound-waves, you know, absolute silence, although" (he went on and everybody giggled) "I have had them used against me at times!"

"I would use one against your campaigns all the time,"

said Iris, joining them. "See, I cut my hair! Isn't it *fun?*" and with a sudden jerk she swung her head down at Alyx to show her short, silver hair, swinging it back and forth and giggling hysterically while Gavrily laughed and tried to catch at it. They were all between two and two-and-a-half meters tall. It was intolerable. They were grabbing at Iris's hair and explaining to each other about the different frazzles they had used and the sound-baffles of the apartments they had been in, and simulated forests with walls that went *tweet-tweet* and how utterly lag it was to install free-fall in your bath-room (if only you could afford it) and take a bath in a bubble, though you must be careful not to use *too* large a bubble or you might suffocate. She dove be-tween them, unnoticed, into the snow where Machine practiced shooting bolts at a target, his eyes hooded in lenses, his ears muffled, his feet never moving. He was on his way to becoming a master. There was a sudden rise in the excited gabble from inside, and turning, Alyx saw someone come out of the far wall with the lieutenant, the first blond person she had seen so far, for everyone except the lieutenant seemed to be some kind of indeterminate, mixed racial type, except for Maudey and Iris, who had what Alyx would have called a dash of the Asiatic. Everyone was a little darker than herself and a little more pronounced in feature, as if they had crossbred in a hundred ways to even out at last, but here came the lieutenant with what Alyx would have called a freak Northman, another giant (she did not give a damn), and then left him inside and came out and sat down on the outside bench.

"Lieutenant," said Alyx, "why are you sending me on this picnic?"

He made a vague gesture, looking back into the shed, fidgeting like a man who has a hundred things to do and cannot make up his mind where to start.

"An explorer," said the lieutenant, "amateur. Very famous."

"Why don't you send them with him and stop this nonsense, then!" she exploded.

"It's not nonsense," he said. "Oh, no."

"Isn't it? A ten-day walk over those foothills? No large predators? An enemy that doesn't give a damn about us? A path a ten-year-old could follow. An explorer right to hand. *And how much do I cost?*"

"Agent," said the lieutenant, "I know civilians," and he looked back in the shed again, where the newcomer had seized Iris and was kissing her, trying to get his hands inside her suit while Gavrily danced around the couple. Maudey was chatting with Raydos, who made sketches on a pad. "Maybe, Agent," said the lieutenant, very quietly, "I know how much you cost, and maybe it is very important to get these people out of here before one of them is killed, and maybe, Agent, there is more to it than that when you take people away from their—from their electromagnetic spectrum, shall we say. That man" (and he indicated the blond) "has never been away from a doctor and armor and helpers and vehicles and cameras in his life." He looked down into the snow. "I shall have to take their drugs away from them," he said. "They won't like that. They are going to walk on their own feet for two hundred and forty kilometers. That may be ten days to you but you will see how far you get with them. You cost more than you think, Agent, and let me tell you something else" (here he lifted his face intently) "which may help you to understand, and that is, Agent, that this is the first time the Trans-Temporal Authority—which is a military authority, thanks be for that—has ever transported any-one from the past for any purpose whatsoever. And that was accidental—I can't explain that now. All this talk about Agents here and Agents there is purely mythologi-cal, fictional, you might say, though why people insist on these silly stories I don't know, for there is only one Agent and that is the first and the last Agent and that, Agent—is you. But don't try to tell them. They won't believe you."

"Is that why you're beginning with a picnic?" said Alyx.

"It will not be a picnic," he said and he looked at the snow again, at Machine's tracks, at Machine, who stood patiently sending bolt after bolt into the paint-sprayed target, his eyes and nose and ears shut to the whole human world.

"What will happen to you?" said Alyx, finally.

"I?" said the young officer. "Oh, I shall die! but that's nothing to you," and he went back into the shed im-mediately, giving instructions to what Iris had called androids, clapping the giant Northerner on the back,

20

calling Alyx to come in. "This is Gunnar," he said. They
shook hands. It seemed an odd custom to Alyx and
apparently to everyone else, for they sniggered. He
flashed a smile at everyone as the pack was fitted onto
his back. "Here," he said, holding out a box, "*Cannabis*,"
and Iris, making a face, handed over a crumpled bun-
dle of her green cylinders. "I hope I don't have to give
these up," said Raydos quietly, stowing his sketchbook
into his pack. "They are not power tools, you know,"
and he watched dispassionately while Maudey argued
for a few minutes, looked a bit sulky and finally produced a tiny, ornate orange cylinder. She took a sniff
from it and handed it over to the lieutenant. Iris looked
malicious. Gavrily confessed he had nothing. The nuns,
of course, said everybody, had nothing and would not
carry weapons. Everyone had almost forgotten about
them. They all straggled out into the snow to where
Machine was picking up the last of his bolts. He turned
to face them, like a man who would be contaminated
by the very air of humankind, nothing showing under
the hood of his suit but his mouth and the goggled lenses
and snout of another species.

"I must have that, too," said Alyx, planting both
feet on the ground.

"Well, after all," said Maudey, "you can't expect—"

"Teach the young fellow a lesson!" said Gavrily.

"Shall I take it off?" remarked the amateur explorer
(*And actor,* thought Alyx) striding forward, smile flashing while Machine bent slowly for the last of his bolts,

fitting it back into the carrying case, not looking at anyone or hearing anything, for all she knew, off on station N-O-T-H-I-N-G twenty-four hours each Earth day, the boy who called himself Machine because he hated the lot of them.

"If you touch him," said Alyx evenly, "I shall kill you," and as they gasped and giggled (Gunnar gave a rueful smile; he had been outplayed) she walked over to him and held out her hand. The boy took off his Trivia and dropped it into the snow; the showing of any face would have been a shock but his was completely denuded of hair, according (she supposed) to the fashion he followed: eyebrows, eyelashes and scalp, and his eyes were a staring, brilliant, shattering, liquescent blue. "You're a good shot," she said. He was not interested. He looked at them without the slightest emotion. "He hardly *ever* talks," said Maudey. They formed a straggling line, walking off toward the low hills and Alyx, a thought suddenly coming to her, said off-handedly before she knew it, "You're mother and daughter, aren't you?"

The entire line stopped. Maudey had instantly turned away, Iris looked furiously angry, Gunnar extremely surprised and only Raydos patiently waited, as usual, watching them all. Machine remained Machine. The nuns were hiding their mouths, shocked, with both hands.

"I thought—"

"If you must—"

"Don't you ever—!"

The voices came at her from all sides.

"Shut up," she said, "and march. I'll do worse yet." The column began again. "Faster," she said. "You know," she added cruelly, carefully listening for the effect of her words, "one of you may die." Behind her there was a stiffening, a gasp, a terrified murmur at such bad, bad taste. "Yes, yes," she said, hammering it in, "one of us may very well die before this trip is over," and quickened her pace in the powdery snow, the even, crisp, shallow snow, as easy to walk in as if put down expressly for a pleasure jaunt, a lovely picnic under the beautiful blue heaven of this best of all possible tourist resorts. "Any one of us," she repeated carefully, "any one of us at all," and all of a sudden she thought *Why, that's true. That's very true.* She sighed. "Come on," she said.

At first she had trouble keeping up with them; then, as they straggled and loitered, she had no trouble at all; and finally they had trouble keeping up with her. The joking and bantering had stopped. She let them halt fairly early (the lieutenant had started them out—wisely, she thought—late in the afternoon) under an overhanging rock. Mountains so old and smooth should not have many caves and outflung walls where a climbing party can rest, but the mountains of Paradise had them. The late, late shadows were violet blue and the sunlight going up the farthest peaks went up like the sunlight in a children's book, with a purity and perfection of color changing into color and the snow melting into cobalt evening which Alyx watched with—

Wonder. Awe. Suspicion. But nobody was about. However, they were making trouble when she got back. They were huddled together, rather irritable, talking insatiably as if they had to make up for their few silent hours in the afternoon's march. It was ten degrees below freezing and would not drop much lower at this time of year, the lieutenant had promised, even though there might be snow, a fact (she thought) for which they might at least look properly thankful.

"Well?" she said, and everyone smiled.

"We've been talking," said Maudey brightly. "About what to do."

"What to do what?" said Alyx.

"What to do next," said Gavrily, surprised. "What else?"

The two nuns smiled.

"We think," said Maudey, "that we ought to go much more slowly and straight across, you know, and Gunnar wants to take photographs—"

"Manual," said the explorer, flashing his teeth.

"And not through the mountains," said Maudey. "It's so up-and-down, you know."

"And *hard*," said Iris.

"And we voted," said Maudey, "and Gunnar won."

"Won what?" said Alyx.

"Well, *won*," said Gavrily, "you know."

"Won what?" repeated Alyx, a little sharply; they

24

all looked embarrassed, not (she thought, surprised) for themselves but for her. Definitely for her.

"They want Gunnar to lead them." No one knew who had spoken. Alyx looked from one to the other but they were as surprised as she; then she whirled around sharply, for it was Machine who had spoken, Machine who had never before said one word. He squatted in the snow, his back against the rock, looking past them. He spoke precisely and without the slightest inflection.

"Thank you," said Alyx. "Is that what you all want?"

"Not I," said Raydos.

"I do," said Maudey.

"And I do," said Iris. "I think—"

"I do," said Gavrily.

"We think—" the nuns began.

She was prepared to blast their ears off, to tell them just what she thought of them. She was shaking all over. She began in her own language, however, and had to switch clumsily into theirs, trying to impress upon them things for which she could not find words, things for which she did not believe the language had words at all: that she was in charge of them, that this was not a pleasure party, that they might die, that it was her job to be responsible for them, and that whoever led them, or how, or why, or in what way, was none of their business. She kept saying it over and over that it was none of their business.

"Oh, everything is everybody's business," said Gavrily cheerfully, as if her feeling that way were quite natural, quite wrong and also completely irrelevant, and they all began to chat again. Gunnar came up to her sympathetically and took hold of her hands. She twisted in his grasp, instinctively beginning a movement that would have ended in the pit of his stomach, but he grasped each of her wrists, saying "No, no, you're not big enough," and holding her indulgently away from him with his big, straight, steady arms. He had begun to laugh, saying "I know this kind of thing too, you see!" when she turned in his grip, taking hold of his wrists in the double hold used by certain circus performers, and bearing down sharply on his arms (he kept them steady for just long enough, thinking he was still holding her off) she lifted herself up as if on a gate, swung under his guard and kicked him right under the arch of the ribs. Luckily the suit cushioned the blow a little. The silence that followed—except for his gasping —was complete. They had never, she supposed, seen Gunnar on the ground that way before. Or anyone else. Then Maudey threw up.

"I am sorry," said Alyx, "but I cannot talk to you. You will do as I say," and she walked away from them and sat down near Machine, whose eyes had never left the snow in front of him, who was making furrows in it with one hand. She sat there, listening to the frightened whispers in back of her, knowing she had behaved badly and wanting to behave even worse all over again, trembling from head to foot with rage, knowing they were only children, cursing herself abominably—and the Trans-Temporal Authority—and her own idiot helplessness and the "commercial war," whatever that might be, and each one of her charges, individually and collectively, until the last of the unfamiliar stars came out and the sky turned black. She fell asleep in her wonderful insulated suit, as did they all, thinking *Oh, God, not even keeping a watch*, and not caring; but she woke from time to time to hear their secure breathing, and then the refrain of a poem came to her in the language of Phoenician Tyre, those great traders who had gone even to the gates of Britain for tin, where the savages painted themselves blue and believed stones to be sacred, not having anything else, the poor bastards. The refrain of the poem was *What will become of me?* which she changed to *What will become of them?* until she realized that nothing at all would become of them, for they did not have to understand her. *But I*, she thought, *will have to understand them.*

And then, sang the merchants of Tyre, that great city, *what, O God, will become of me?*

She had no trouble controlling them the next day; they were much too afraid of her. Gunnar, however, plainly admired her and this made her furious. She was getting into her stride now, over the easy snow, getting used to the pack resting on some queer contraption not on her back but on her hips, as they all did, and finding the snow easy to walk over. The sun of Paradise shone in an impossibly blue sky, which she found upsetting. But the air was good; the air was wonderful. She was getting used to walking. She took to outpacing them, long-legged as they were, and sitting in the snow twenty meters away, cross-legged like a monk, until they caught up, then watching them expressionlessly—like a trail-marker—until they passed her, casting back looks that were far from pleasant; and then repeating the whole thing all over again. After the noon meal she stopped that; it was too cruel. They sat down in the middle of a kind of tilted wasteland—it was the side of a hill but one's up-and-down got easily mixed in the mountains—and ate everything in the plastic bags marked Two-B, none of it dried and all of it magnificent; Alyx had never had such food in her life on a trip before: fruits and spicy little buns, things like sausages, curls of candy that sprung round your finger and smelled of ginger, and for drinking, the bags you filled with snow and hung inside your suit to melt. Chilly, but efficient. She ate half of everything and put the rest back, out of habit. With venomous looks, everybody else ate everything. "She's tinier than we are," Gunnar said, trying to smooth things over, "and I'm sure there's more than enough!" Alyx reached inside her suit and scratched one arm. "There may not be enough," she said, "can't tell," and returned the rest to her pack, wondering why you couldn't trust adults to eat one meal at a time without marking it with something. She could not actually read the numbers. But perhaps it was a custom or a ritual. *A primitive ritual,* she thought. She was in much better spirits. *A primitive ritual,* she repeated to herself, *practiced through inveterate and age-old super-*

stition. She dearly longed to play with the curly candy again. She suddenly remembered the epigram made one Mediterranean evening by the Prince of Tyre on the palace roof over a game of chess and began spontaneously to tell it to them, with all that had accompanied it: the sails in the bay hanging disembodied and white like the flowers in the royal garden just before the last light goes, the smell of the bay at low tide, not as bad as inlanders think but oddly stimulating, bringing to one's mind the complex processes of decay and life, the ins and outs of things, the ins and outs of herself who could speak six dialects from the gutter to the palace, and five languages, one of them the old Egyptian; and how she had filched the rather valuable chess set later, for the Tyrians were more than a little ostentatious despite their reputation for tough-mindedness, odd people, the adventurers, the traders, the merchants of the Mediterranean, halfway in their habits between the cumbersome dignities of royal Egypt and the people of Crete, who knew how to live if anyone ever had, decorating their eggshell-thin bowls with sea-creatures made unbelievably graceful or with musicians lying in beds of anemones and singing and playing on the flute. She laughed and quoted the epigram itself, which had been superb, a double pun in two languages, almost a pity to deprive a man like that of a chess set worth—

Nobody was listening. She turned around and stared at them. For a moment she could not think, only smell and stare, and then something shifted abruptly inside her head and she could name them again: Gunnar, Machine, Raydos, Maudey, Iris, Gavrily, the two nuns. She had been talking in her own language. They shambled along, leaning forward against the pull of the hippacks, ploughing up the snow in their exhaustion, these huge, soft people to whom one could not say anything of any consequence. Their faces were drawn with fatigue. She motioned them to stop and they toppled down into the snow without a word, Iris's cheek right in the cold stuff itself and the two nuns collapsed across each other in a criss-cross. They had worn, she believed, a symbol on a chain around their necks something like the symbol . . . but she did not want to fall back into her own speech again. She felt extremely stupid. "I am sorry that you're tired," she said.

"No, no," muttered Gunnar, his legs straight out in the snow, staring ahead.

"We'll take a break," she said, wondering where the phrase had come from all of a sudden. The sun was hardly halfway down in the sky. She let them rest for an hour or more until they began to talk; then she forced them to their feet and began it all again, the nightmare of stumbling, slipping, sliding, the unmistakable agonies of plodding along with cramped legs and a drained body, the endless pull of the weight at one's back. . . . She remembered what the lieutenant had said about people deprived of their electromagnetic spectrum. Long before nightfall she stopped them and let them revive while she scouted around for animal tracks—or human tracks—or anything—but found nothing. Paradise was a winter sportsman's—well, paradise. She asked about animals, but nobody knew for certain or nobody was telling, although Gunnar volunteered the information that Paradise had not been extensively mapped. Maudey complained of a headache. They ate again, this time from a bag marked Two-C, still with nothing dried (*Why carry all that weight in water?* Alyx thought, remembering how the desert people could ride for weeks on nothing but ground wheat), stowed empty, deflated Two-C into their packs and lay down— right in the middle of a vast, empty snow-field. It gave them all the chills. Alyx lay a little apart, to let them talk about her as she was sure they would, and then crept closer. They were talking about her. She made a face and retreated again. A little later she got them up and into the hills above until at sunset it looked as if they would have to sleep in the open. She left them huddled together and went looking about for a cave, but found nothing, until, coming around the path at the edge of a rather sharp drop, she met Machine coming the other way.

"What the devil—!" she exclaimed, planting herself in his way, arms akimbo, face tilted up to look into his.

"Cave," he said blandly and walked up the side of the hill with his long legs, around above her, and down on to the path. He even got back to the others faster than she did, though sweat was running from under his hood.

"All right," said Alyx as she rejoined them, "it's found a cave," but she found them all standing up ready to

31

go, most yawning, all trying not to stagger, and Gunnar beaming heartily in a way that made her wish she had hit him lower down, much lower down, when she had the chance. *Professional,* she thought. "He told us," said Maudey with her head in the air, "before you came," and the troop of them marched—more or less—after the bald-headed boy, who had found a shallow depression in the rock where they could gather in relative comfort. If there had been a wind, although there was no wind on Paradise, the place would have sheltered them; if it had been snowing, although it was not snowing on Paradise, the place would have protected them; and if anyone had been looking for them, although apparently no one was, the place would have afforded a partial concealment. They all got together; they sat down; some of them threw back their hoods; and then they began to talk. They talked and talked and talked. They discussed whether Maudey had behaved impatiently towards Iris, or whether Iris had tried to attract Gunnar, or whether the nuns were participating enough in the group interaction, with due allowance made for their religious faith, of course, and whether the relationship between Raydos and Gunnar was competitive, and what Gavrily felt about the younger men, and whether he wanted to sleep with Iris, and on and on and on about how they felt about each other and how they ought to feel about each other and how they had felt about each other with an insatiability that stunned Alyx and a wealth of detail that fascinated her, considering that all these interactions had been expressed by people staggering with fatigue, under a load of eleven kilos per person, and exposed to a great deal of unaccustomed exercise. She felt sorry for Machine. She wished she had a Trivia herself. She lay at the mouth of the cave until she could not stand it; then she retreated to the back and lay on her stomach until her elbows galled her; then she took off into the snow in front of the cave where there was a little light and lay on her back, watching the strange stars.

"We do it all the time, I'm afraid," said a man's voice beside her. *Raydos*, she thought instantly. *Machine would have said "they."*

"It doesn't—" he went on, "it doesn't mean—well, it doesn't mean anything, really. It's a kind of habit."

She said nothing.

"I came out," he said, "to apologize for us and to ask you about the watch. I've explained it to the others. I will take the first watch.

"I have read about such things," he added proudly.

Still she said nothing.

"I wish you would repeat to me," he went on slowly, and she realized he was trying to talk simply to her, "what you said this morning in the other language."

"I can't," she said, and then she added, feeling stupid, "the witty saying of . . . of the Prince of Tyre."

"The epigram," he said patiently.

"Epigram," she repeated.

"What did the Prince of Tyre say?"

"He said," she translated, feeling her way desperately,

"that in any . . . time . . . any time you . . . have something, whatever tendencies—whatever factors in a situation you have, whatever of these can—can unpredict—"

"Can go wrong," said he.

"Can go wrong," she parroted, caught halfway between two worlds. "Can wrong itself. It—" but here
the man beside her burst into such a roar of laughter
that she turned to look at him.

"The proverbial Third Law," he said. "Whatever can
go wrong, will," and he burst into laughter again. He
was big, but they were all big; in the faint glimmer of
the snow-field . . .

His hood was back; his hair was pale.

Gunnar.

Alone once more, she lay several meters farther out
with her arms wrapped about herself, thinking a bit sav-
agely that the "witty saying" of His Highness had been
expressed in two words, not five, both of them punning,
both rhymed and each with a triple internal assonance
that exactly contrasted with the other.

Damned barbarians! she snapped to herself, and fell
asleep.

The next day it began to snow, the soft, even snow
of Paradise, hiding their footprints and the little bags
of excrement they buried here and there. The insulated
suits were ingenious. Her people began to talk to her,
just a little, condescendingly but trying to be affable,
more and more cheerful as they neared Point B, where

they would need her no more, where she could dwindle into a memory, an anecdote, a party conversation: "Did you know, I once met the most *fascinating*—" They really had very little imagination, Alyx thought. In their place she would be asking everything: where she came from, who she was, how she lived, the desert people who worshiped the wind god, what the Tyrians ate, their economic system, their families, their beliefs, their feelings, their clothes, the Egyptians, the Minoans, how the Minoans made those thin, dyed bowls, how they traded ostrich eggs and perfumes from Egypt, what sort of ships they sailed, how it felt to rob a house, how it felt to cut a throat. . . . But all they did was talk about themselves.

"You ought to have cosmetic surgery," said Maudey. "I've had it on my face and my breasts. It's ingenious. Of course I had a good doctor. And you have to be careful dyeing eyebrows and eyelashes, although the genetic alterations are usually pretty stable. But they might *spread*, you know. Can you imagine having a *blue forehead?*"

"I ran away from home," said Iris, "at the age of fifteen and joined a Youth Core. Almost everyone has Youth Cores, although mine wasn't a delinquent Youth Core and some people will tell you that doesn't count. But let me tell you, it changed my life. It's better than hypnotic psychotherapy. They call it a Core because it forms the core of your adolescent rebellion, don't you see, and I would have been nobody without it, absolutely nobody, it changed my whole life and all my values. Did you ever run away from home?"

"Yes," said Alyx. "I starved."

"Nobody starves any more," said Iris. "A Youth Core to fit each need. I joined a middle-status Youth Core. Once you're past fourteen you needn't drag—um—your family into everything. We forget about that. It's much better."

"Some people call me a Conamon," said Gavrily, "but where would we be without them? There are commercial wars and wars; you know all about that. The point is there are no more wars. I mean real wars. That would be a terrible thing. And if you get caught in a commercial war, it's your own fault, you see. Mixed interests. Mixed economy. I deal in people. Sounds bad, doesn't it? Some people would say I manage people, but I say I help them. I work *with* them. I form values. Can you imagine what it would be like without us? No one to bring your group interests to. No one to mediate between you and the army or you and business or you and government. Why, there wouldn't *be* any local government, really, though of course I'm not Gov; I'm Con. Mixed interests. It's the only way."

"Wrap-arounds!" said Raydos contemptuously. "Anybody can build a wrap-around. Simplest thing in the world. The problem is to recover the purity of the medium—I hope I'm not boring you—and to recover the purity of the medium you have to withdraw within its boundaries, not stretch them until they crack. I've done environments until I'm sick of them. I want something you can walk around, not something that walks around you. Lights geared to heartbeats, drug combinations, vertigo—I'm through with all that; it's mere vulgarity. Have you ever tried to draw something? Just draw something? Wait a minute; stand still." (And he sketched a few lines on a piece of paper.) "There! *That's* avant-garde for you!"

"The consciousness," said the nuns, speaking softly one after the other, "must be expanded to include the All. That is the only true church. Of course, that is what *we* believe. We do not wish to force our beliefs on others. We are the ancient church of consciousness and Buddha, nearly six hundred years old; I do hope that when we get back you'll attend a service with us. Sex is only part of the ceremony. The drugs are the main part. Of course we're not using them now, but we do carry them. The lieutenant knew we would never touch them. Not while there's the possibility of violence. The essence of violence violates consciousness while the consciousness of expanded consciousness correlates with the essence of the All which is Love, extended Love and the deepening and expanding of experience implied by the consciousness-expanded consciousness."

"You *do* understand," they chorused anxiously, "don't you?"

"Yes," said Alyx, "perfectly."

Gunnar talked passionately about electronics.

"Now there must be some way," he said, "to neutralize this electromagnetic watch-grid they've set up or to polarize it. Do you think polarization would ring the alarm? It might be damn fun! We're only behaving like parts of the landscape now—you *will* stop me if you don't understand, won't you—but there must be regions in the infra-bass where the shock waves—damn! Paradise doesn't have faults and quakes—well, then, the ultra-hard—they must have the cosmic rays down to the twentieth place—somehow— If I had only brought —you know, I think I could rig up some kind of interference—of course they'd spot that—but just think of the equipment—"

Machine said nothing at all. She took to walking with Machine. They walked through the soft, falling snow of Paradise in absolute silence under a sky that dropped feathers like the sky in a fairy tale, like a sky she had never seen before that made endless pillows and hummocks of the rounded stones of Paradise, stones just large enough to sit on, as if someone had been before them all the way providing armchairs and tables. Machine was very restful. On the tenth day she took his arm and leaned against him briefly; on the eleventh day he said:

"Where do you come from?"

"I come," she said softly, "from great cities and palaces and back-alleys and cemeteries and rotten ships.

"And where," she added, "do you come from?"

"Nowhere!" said Machine—and he spat on the snow.

On the sixteenth day of their ten-day journey they found Base B. Everyone had been excited all day—"picnicky" Alyx called it. Maudey had been digging her fingers into her hair and lamenting the absence of something called an electric tease; Gavrily was poking both women, a little short of breath; and Gunnar displayed his smile—that splendid smile—a little too often to be accounted for by the usual circumstances and laughed a good deal to himself.

"Oh golly, oh gosh, oh golly, oh golly, oh gosh!" sang Iris.

"Is that what they taught you at your Core?" said Raydos dryly.

"Yes," said Iris sniffishly. "*Do* you mind?" and she went on singing the words while Raydos made a face. "Didn't you go to a Core?" said Iris and when Raydos informed her that he had gone to a School (whatever that was) instead, Iris sang "Oh golly, oh gosh" so loud that Alyx told her to stop.

"Animals don't sing," said Alyx.

"Well, I hope you're not being moralistic—" Iris began.

"Animals," said Alyx, "don't sing. People sing. People can be caught. People can be killed. Stop singing."

"But we're so near," said Gunnar.

"Come on," said Gavrily. He began to run. Maudey was shepherding the nuns, chattering excitedly; everything was there—the line of boulders, the hill, a little dip in the snow, up another hill (a steep one this time) and there was Base B. Everybody could go home now. It was all over. They ran up to the top of the hill and nearly tumbled over one another in confusion, Gavrily with his arms spread out against the sky, one of the

39

nuns fallen on one knee and Iris nearly knocking Maudey over.

Base B was gone. In the little dell where there should have been a metal shed with a metal door leading underground, to safety, to home, to the Army, to a room where the ceiling whirled so familiarly ("a little bit of home") and coiled thingamajigs which ate whatever you dropped on the grassy floor, there was no metal shed and no metal door. There was something like a splotch of metal foil smashed flat and a ragged hole in the middle of it, and as they watched, something indeterminate came out of the hole. There was a faint noise in the sky.

"Scatter!" cried Alyx. "Down on your knees!" and as they stood there gaping, she slammed the three nearest across the face and then the others so that when the air vehicle—no one looked up to get a clear view of it—came barreling over the horizon, they were all down on their hands and knees, pretending to be animals. Alyx got down just in time. When the thing had gone, she dared to look into the dell again, where the indeterminate thing had split into four things, which stood at the edges of an exact square while a box the size of a small room floated slowly down between them. The moment it landed they burrowed into it, or were taking it apart; she could not tell. "Lie flat," said Alyx softly. "Don't talk. Gunnar, use your binoculars." *No decent knife,* she thought wryly, *not even a fire, but these marvelous things we do have.*

"I don't see—" began Iris spiritedly.

"Shut up," said Alyx. He was focusing the binoculars.

She knew about lenses because she had learned to do it with her own pair. Finally he took them away from his eyes and stared for a few moments into the snow. Then he said, "You can stand up now."

"Is it safe?" cried one of the nuns. "Can we go down now?"

"The snow makes it hard to see," said Gunnar slowly, "but I do not think so. No, I do not think so. Those are commercial usuforms, unpacking a food storage container. They are not Army. Army never uses commercial equipment."

"I think," he said, "that Base B has been taken," and he began quite openly and unashamedly to cry. The snow of Paradise (for it had begun to snow) fell on his cheeks and mingled with his tears, fell as beautifully as feathers from pillows, as if Hera were shaking out the feather quilts of Heaven while the amateur explorer cried and the seven people who had looked to him as their last hope looked first at each other—but there was no help there—and finally—hesitantly—but frightened, oh were they frightened!—at Alyx.

"All right," she said, "it's my show.

"Come on, come on!" she snapped, with all the contempt she could muster, "what's the matter with the lot of you? You're not dead; you're not paralyzed; look alive, will you? I've been in tighter spots than this and I've come out; you there" (she indicated Machine) "pinch them awake, will you! Oh, *will* you snap out of it!" and she shook Gunnar violently, thinking him the most likely

41

to have already recovered. He, at least, had cried. She felt surrounded by enormous puppies.

"Yes—yes—I'm all right," he said at last.

"Listen," she said, "I want to know about those things. When will there be another air vehicle?"

"I don't know," he said.

"How long will it take them to unpack, unload, whatever?"

"About . . . about an hour, I think," he said.

"Then there won't be another box for an hour," she said. "How far can they see?"

"See?" said Gunnar helplessly.

"How far can they perceive, then?" persisted Alyx. "Perceive, you idiot, look, see, hear, touch—what the devil, you know what I mean!"

"They—they perceive," said Gunnar slowly, taking a deep breath, "at about three meters. Four meters. They're meant for close work. They're a low form."

"How do you kill them?"

He indicated the center of his chest.

"Can we do it with a crossbow?" she said.

"Ye-es," he said, "very close range, but—"

"Good. If one of them goes, what happens?"

"I'm not sure," he said, sitting up abruptly. "I think nothing would happen for a few seconds. They've—" (he lifted the binoculars to his eyes again) "they've established some kind of unloading pattern. They seem to be working pretty independently. That model—if it is that model—would let one of them lie maybe fifteen-twenty seconds before radioing down for a removal . . .

Perhaps longer. They might simply change the pattern."

"And if all four went dead?"

"Why, nothing would happen," he said, "nothing at all. Not—not for about half an hour. Maybe more. Then they'd begin to wonder downstairs why the stuff wasn't coming in. But we do have half an hour."

"So," said Alyx, "you come with me. And Machine. And—"

"I'll come!" said Iris, clasping her hands nervously. Alyx shook her head. "If you're discriminating against me," said Iris wonderingly, "because I'm a *girl*—"

"No, dear, you're a lousy shot," said Alyx. "Gunnar, you take that one; Machine, that one; I take two. All of you! If they fall and nothing happens, you come down that slope like hell and if something does happen, you go the other way twice as fast! We need food. I want dried stuff, light stuff; you'll recognize it, I won't. Everything you can carry. And keep your voices down. Gunnar, what's—"

"Calories," said Machine.

"Yes, yes, lots of that," said Alyx impatiently, "that—that stuff. Come on," and she started down the slope, waving the other two to circle the little dell. Piles of things—they could not see very well through the falling snow—were growing on each side of the box. The box seemed to be slowly collapsing. The moving things left strange tracks, half-human, half-ploughed; she crossed one of them where a thing had wandered up the side of the hollow for some reason of its own. She hoped they did not do that often. She found her bare hands

43

sweating on the stock of the bow, her gloves hanging from her wrists; *if only they had been men!* she thought, and not things that could call for help in a silent voice called radio, or fall down and not be dead, or you didn't know whether they were dead or not. Machine was in position. Gunnar raised his bow. They began to close in silently and slowly until Gunnar stopped; then she sighted on the first and shot. They were headless, with a square protuberance in the middle of the "chest" and an assemblage of many coiled arms that ended in pincers, blades, hooks, what looked like plates. It went down, silently. She turned for the second, carefully reloading the bow, only to find Machine waving and grinning. He had got two. The fourth was also flat on the ground. They ran towards the big box, Alyx involuntarily closing her eyes as she passed the disabled things; then they leaned against the big box, big as a room. Piles of boxes, piles of plastic bladders, bags, cartons, long tubes, stoppers, things that looked like baby round cheese. She waved an arm in the air violently. The others came running, skidding, stumbling down the slope. They began to pick up things under Gunnar's direction and stuff them into each other's packs, whispering a little, talking endlessly, while Alyx squatted down in the snow and kept her bow trained dead-steady on that hole in the ground. There was probably not much sense in doing so, but she did it anyway. She was convinced it was the proper thing to do. Someone was enthusiastically stuffing something into her pack; "Easy, easy," she said, and sighted on that hole in the ground, keeping her aim decent and listening for any improper sounds from above or below until someone said in her ear, "We're done," and she took off immediately up the slope, not looking back. It took the others several minutes to catch up with her. *Thank God it's snowing!* she thought. She counted them. It was all right.

"Now!" she gasped. "We're going into the mountains. Double quick!" and all the rest of the day she pushed them until they were ready to drop, up into the foothills among the increasingly broken rocks where they had to scramble on hands and knees and several people tore holes in their suits. The cold got worse. There were gusts of wind. She took them the long way round, by pure instinct, into the worst kind of country, the place where no one trying to get anywhere—or trying to escape—would go, in a strange, doubled, senseless series of turns and re-turns, crossing their path once, up over obstacles and then in long, leisurely curves on the flattest part of the hills. She kept carefully picturing their relation to the abandoned Base B, telling herself *They'll know someone was there;* and then repeating obsessively *Part of the landscape. Part of the landscape* and driving them all the harder, physically shoving them along, striking them, prodding them, telling them in the ugliest way she could that they would die, that they would be eaten, that their minds would be picked, that they would be crippled, deformed, tortured, that they would die, that they would die, die, die, and finally that she would kill them herself if they stopped, if they stopped for a moment, kill them, scar their faces for life, disembowel them, and finally she had to all but torture them herself, bruise them and pinch them in the nerves she alone knew about until it was less painful to go on than to be goaded constantly, to be terrified, to be slapped and threatened and beaten. At sundown she let them collapse out in the open and slept immediately herself. Two hours later she woke up. She shook Gunnar.

"Gunnar!" she said. He came awake with a kind of convulsive leap, struggling horribly. She put an arm around him, crawling tiredly through the snow and leaned against him to quiet him. She felt herself slipping off again and jerked awake. He had his head in both hands, pressing his temples and swinging his head from side to side.

"Gunnar!" she said, "you are the only one who knows anything about this place. Where do we go?"

"All right, all right," he said. He was swaying a little. She reached under the cuff of his suit and pinched the skin on the inside of his forearm; his eyes opened and he looked at her.

"Where . . . what?" he said.

"Where do we go? Is there any neutral area in this— this place?"

"One moment," he said, and he put his head in his hands again. Then he looked up, awake. "I know," he said, "that there is a control Embassy somewhere here. There is always at least one. It's Military, not Gov; you wouldn't understand that but it doesn't matter. We'd be safe there."

"Where is it?" she said.

"I think," he said, "that I know where it is. It's nearer the Pole, I think. Not too far. A few hours by aircraft, I think. Three hours."

"How long," said she, "on foot?"

"Oh," he said, slipping down into the snow onto one arm, "maybe—maybe twice this. Or a little more. Say five hundred kilometers."

"How long," said she insistently, "is that?"

"Oh not much," he said, yawning and speaking fuzzily. "Not much . . . two hours by aircraft." He smiled. "You might have heard it called," he said, "three hundred *miles*, I think. Or a little less." And he rolled over on his side and went to sleep.

Well, that's not so bad, she thought, half asleep, forgetting them all for the moment and thinking only of herself. *Fourteen, fifteen days, that's all. Not bad.* She looked around. Paradise had begun to blow up a little, covering the farthest of her charges with drifts of snow: eight big, fit people with long, long legs. *Oh God of Hell!* she thought suddenly. *Can I get them to do ten miles a day? Is it three hundred miles? A month? Four hundred? And food—!* so she went and kicked Machine awake, telling him to keep the first watch, then call Iris, and have Iris call her.

"You know," she said, "I owe you something."

He said nothing, as usual.

"When I say 'shoot one,' " said Alyx, "I mean shoot one, not two. Do you understand?"

Machine smiled slightly, a smile she suspected he had spent many years in perfecting: cynical, sullen, I-can-do-it-and-you-can't smile. A thoroughly nasty look. She said:

"You stupid bastard, I might have killed you by accident trying to make that second shot!" and leaning forward, she slapped him backhanded across the face, and then the other way forehand as a kind of afterthought because she was tired. She did it very hard. For a moment his face was only the face of a young man, a soft face, shocked and unprotected. Tears sprang to his eyes. Then he began to weep, turning his face away and putting it down on his knees, sobbing harder and harder, clutching at his knees and pressing his face between them to hide his cries, rocking back and forth, then lying on his face with his hands pressed to his eyes, crying out loud to the stars. He subsided slowly, sobbing, calming down, shaken by less and less frequent spasms of tears, and finally was quiet. His face was wet. He lay back in the snow and stretched out his arms, opening his hands loosely as if he had finally let go of something. He smiled at her, quite genuinely. He looked as if he loved her. "Iris," he said.

"Yes, baby," she said, "Iris," and walked back to her place before anything else could happen. There was a neutral place up there—somewhere—if they could find it—where they would be taken in—if they could make it—and where they would be safe—if they could get to it. If they lived.

And if only they don't drown me between the lot of them, she thought irrationally. And fell asleep.

Paradise was not well mapped, as she found out the next morning with Gunnar's help. He did not know the direction. She asked him about the stars and the sun and the time of year, doing some quick calculating, while everyone else tumbled the contents of their packs into the snow, sorting food and putting it back with low-toned remarks that she did not bother to listen to. The snow had lightened and Paradise had begun to blow up a little with sharp gusts that made their suit jackets flap suddenly now and again.

"Winter has begun," said Alyx. She looked sharply at the explorer. "How cold does it get?"

He said he did not know. They stowed back into their packs the detail maps that ended at Base B (*Very efficient,* she thought) because there was no place to bury them among the rocks. They were entirely useless. The other members of the party were eating breakfast—making faces—and Alyx literally had to stand over them while they ate, shutting each bag or box much against the owner's will, even prying those big hands loose (though they were all afraid of her) and then doling out the food she had saved to all of them. The cold had kept it fairly fresh. She told them they would be traveling for three weeks. She ate a couple of handfuls of some dried stuff herself and decided it was not bad. She was regarded dolefully and sulkily by seven pairs of angry eyes.

"Well?" she said.

"It tastes like—like crams," said Iris.

"It's junk," said Gavrily gravely, "dried breakfast food. Made of grains. And some other things."

"Some of it's hard as rocks," said Maudey.

"That's starch," said Raydos, "dried starch kernels."

"I don't know what dried starch kernels is," said Maudey with energy, "but I know what it tastes like. It tastes like—"

"You will put the dried kennels," said Alyx, "or anything else that is hard-as-rocks in your water bottles, where it will stop being hard as rocks. Double handful, please. That's for dinner."

"What do we eat for lunch?" said Iris.

"More junk," said Raydos. "No?"

"Yes," said Alyx. "More junk."

"Kernels," said Raydos, "by the way," and they all got up from the ground complaining, stiff as boards and aching in the joints. She told them to move about a bit but to be careful how they bent over; then she asked those with the torn suits whether they could mend them. Under the skin of the suits was something like thistledown but very little of it, and under that a layer of something silver. You could really sleep in the damn things. People were applying tape to themselves when there was a noise in the air; all dropped heavily to their hands and knees, some grunting—though not on purpose—and the aircraft passed over in the direction of what Alyx had decided to call the south. The equator, anyway. Far to the south and very fast. *Part of the landscape,* she thought. She got them to their feet again, feeling like a coal-heaver, and praised them, saying they had been very quick. Iris looked pleased. Maudey, who was patching up an arm, did not appear to notice; Gavrily was running a tape-strip down the shoulder of one of the nuns and the other was massaging Raydos's back where he had apparently strained something in getting up or down. He looked uncomfortable and uncaring. Gunnar had the professional smile on his face. *My dog,* she thought. Machine was relieving himself off to one side and kicking snow over the spot. He then came over and lifted one cupped hand to his forehead, as if he were trying to take away a headache, which she did not understand. He looked disappointed.

"That's a salute," said Raydos. He grimaced a little and moved his shoulders.

"A what?" said she.

"Army," said Raydos, moving off and flexing his knees. Machine did it again. He stood there expectantly so she did it, too, bringing up one limp hand to her face and down again. They stood awkwardly, smiling at one another, or not perhaps awkwardly, only waiting, until Raydos stuck his tall head over her shoulder and said, "Army salute. He admires the army. I think he likes you," and Machine turned his back instantly, everything going out of his face.

I cannot, thought Alyx, *tell that bum to shut up merely*

51

for clearing up a simple point. On the other hand, I cannot possibly—and if I have to keep restraining myself—I will not let—I cannot, will not, will not let that interfering fool—

Iris burst into pure song.

"OH, SHUT UP!" shouted Alyx, "FOR GOD'S SAKE!" and marshaled them into some kind of line, abjuring them for Heaven's sake to hurry up and be quiet. She wished she had never gotten into this. She wished three or four of them would die and make it easier for her to keep track of them. She wished several would throw themselves off cliffs. She wished there were cliffs they could throw themselves off of. She was imagining these deaths in detail when one of them loomed beside her and an arm slid into hers. It was Raydos.

"I won't interfere again," he said, "all right?" and then he faded back into the line, silent, uncaring, as if Machine's thoughts had somehow become his own. Perhaps they were swapping minds. It occurred to her that she ought to ask the painter to apologize to the boy, not for interfering, but for talking about him as if he weren't there; then she saw the two of them (she thought it was them) conferring briefly together. Perhaps it had been done. She looked up at the bleary spot in the sky that was the sun and ran down the line, motioning them all to one side, telling them to keep the sun to their left and that Gunnar would show them what constellations to follow that night, if it was clear. Don't wander. Keep your eyes open. Think. Watch it. Machine joined her and walked silently by her side, his eyes on his feet. Paradise, which had sloped gently, began to climb, and they climbed with it, some of them falling down. She went to the head of the line and led them for an hour, then dropped back to allow Gunnar, the amateur mountain-climber, to lead the way. She discussed directions with him. The wind was getting worse. Paradise began to show bare rock. They stopped for a cold and miserable lunch and Alyx saw that everyone's bow was unsprung and packed, except for hers; "Can't have you shooting yourselves in the feet," she said. She told Gunnar it might look less suspicious if. "If," he said. Neither finished the thought. They tramped through the afternoon, colder and colder, with the sun receding early into the mountains, struggled on, climbing slopes that a professional would have laughed at. They found the hoof-prints of something like a goat and Alyx thought *I could live on this country for a year*. She dropped back in the line and joined Machine again, again silent, unspeaking for hours. Then suddenly she said:

"What's a pre-school conditioning director?"

"A teacher," said Machine in a surprisingly serene voice, "of very small children."

"It came into my mind," she said, "all of a sudden, that I was a *pre-school conditioning director*."

"Well, you are," he said gravely, "aren't you?"

He seemed to find this funny and laughed on and off, quietly, for the rest of the afternoon. She did not.

That was the night Maudey insisted on telling the

story of her life. She sat in the half-gloom of the cave they had found, clasping her hands in front of her, and went through a feverish and unstoppable list of her marriages: the line marriage, the double marriage, the trial marriage, the period marriage, the group marriage. Alyx did not know what she was talking about. Then Maudey began to lament her troubles with her unstable self-image and at first Alyx thought that she had no soul and therefore no reflection in a mirror, but she knew that was nonsense; so soon she perceived it was one of *their points* (by then she had taken to classifying certain things as *their points*) and tried not to listen, as all gathered around Maudey and analyzed her self-image, using terms Trans-Temp had apparently left out of Alyx's vocabulary, perhaps on purpose. Gunnar was especially active in the discussion. They crowded around her, talking solemnly while Maudey twisted her hands in the middle, but nobody touched her; it occurred to Alyx that although several of them had touched herself, they did not seem to like to get too close to one another. Then it occurred to her that there was something odd in Maudey's posture and something unpleasantly reminiscent in the breathiness of her voice; she decided Maudey had a fever. She wormed her way into the group and seized the woman by the arm, putting her other hand on Maudey's face, which was indeed unnaturally hot.

"She's sick," said Alyx.

"Oh no," said everybody else.

"She's got a fever," said Alyx.

"No, no," said one of the nuns, "it's the drug."

"What—drug?" said Alyx, controlling her temper. How these people could manage to get into such scrapes—

"It's Re-Juv," said Gavrily. "She's been taking Re-Juv and of course the withdrawal symptoms don't come on for a couple of weeks. But she'll be all right."

"It's an unparalleled therapeutic opportunity," said the other nun. Maudey was moaning that nobody cared about her, that nobody had ever paid any attention to her, and whereas other people's dolls were normal when they were little, hers had only had a limited stock of tapes and could only say the same things over and over, just like a person. She said she had always known it wasn't real. No one touched her. They urged her to integrate this perception with her unstable self-image.

"Are you going," said Alyx, "to let her go on like that *all night?*"

"We wouldn't think of stopping her," said Gavrily in a shocked voice and they all went back to talking. "Why wasn't your doll alive?" said one of the nuns in a soft voice. "Think, now; tell us, why do you feel—" Alyx pushed past two of them to try to touch the woman or take her hand, but at this point Maudey got swiftly up and walked out of the cave.

"Eight gods and seven devils!" shouted Alyx in her own language. She realized a nun was clinging to each arm.

"Please don't be distressed," they said, "she'll come back," like twins in unison, only one actually said "She'll

55

return" and the other "She'll come back." Voices pursued her from the cave, everlastingly those damned voices; she wondered if they knew how far an insane woman could wander in a snowstorm. Insane she was, drug or no drug; Alyx had seen too many people behave too oddly under too many different circumstances to draw unnecessary distinctions. She found Maudey some thirty meters along the rock-face, crouching against it.

"Maudey, you must come back," said Alyx.

"Oh, I know *you*," said Maudey, in a superior tone.

"You will get lost in the snow," said Alyx softly, carefully freeing one hand from its glove, "and you won't be comfortable and warm and get a good night's sleep. Now come along."

Maudey smirked and cowered and said nothing.

"Come back and be comfortable and warm," said Alyx. "Come back and go to sleep. Come, dear; come on, dear," and she caught Maudey's arm with her gloved hand and with the other pressed a blood vessel at the base of her neck. The woman passed out immediately and fell down in the snow. Alyx kneeled over her, holding one arm back against the joint, just in case Maudey should decide to get contentious. *And how*, she thought, *do you get her back now when she weighs twice as much as you, clever one?* The wind gave them a nasty shove, then gusted in the other direction. Maudey was beginning to stir. She was saying something louder and louder; finally Alyx heard it.

"I'm a living doll," Maudey was saying, "I'm a living

doll, I'm a living doll, I'm a living doll" interspersed with terrible sobs.

They do tell the truth, thought Alyx, *sometimes.* "You," she said firmly, "are a woman. A woman. A woman."

"I'm a doll!" cried Maudey.

"You," said Alyx, "are a woman. A woman with dyed hair. A silly woman. But a woman. A woman!"

"No I'm not," said Maudey stubbornly, like an older Iris.

"Oh, you're a damned fool!" snapped Alyx, peering nervously about and hoping that their voices would not attract anything. She did not expect people, but she knew that where there are goats or things like goats there are things that eat the things that are like goats.

"Am I damned?" said Maudey. "What's damned?"

"Lost," said Alyx absently, and slipping her gloved hand free, she lifted the crossbow from its loop on her back, loaded it and pointed it away at the ground. Maudey was wiggling her freed arm, with an expression of pain. "You hurt me," she said. Then she saw the bow and sat up in the snow, terrified, shrinking away.

"Will you shoot me, will you shoot me?" she cried.

"Shoot you?" said Alyx.

"You'll shoot me, you hate me!" wailed Maudey, clawing at the rock-face. "You hate me, you hate me, you'll kill me!"

"I think I will," said Alyx simply, "unless you go back to the cave."

"No, no, no," said Maudey.

"If you don't go back to the cave," said Alyx carefully,

"I am going to shoot you," and she drove the big woman in front of her, step by step, back along the narrow side of the mountain, back on her own tracks that the snow had already half-obliterated, back through Paradise to the opening of the cave. She trained the crossbow on Maudey until the woman stepped into the group of people inside; then she stood there, blocking the entrance, the bow in her hand.

"One of you," she said, "tie her wrists together."

"You are doing incalculable harm," said one of the nuns.

"Machine," she said, "take rope from your pack. Tie that woman's wrists together and then tie them to Gavrily's feet and the nuns' feet and Iris's. Give them plenty of room but make the knots fast."

"I hear and obey," said Raydos dryly, answering for the boy, who was apparently doing what she had told him to.

"You and Raydos and I and Gunnar will stand watch," she said.

"What's there to watch, for heaven's sake," muttered Iris. Alyx thought she probably did not like being connected to Maudey in any way at all, not even for safety.

"Really," said Gavrily, "she would have come back, you know! I think you might try to understand that!"

"I would have come back," said Maudey in a surprisingly clear and sensible tone, "of course I would have come back, don't be silly," and this statement precipitated such a clamor of discussion, vilification, self-justi-

fication and complaints that Alyx stepped outside the
cave with her blood pounding in her ears and her
hands grasping the stock of the crossbow. She asked
the gods to give her strength, although she did not believe in them and never had. Her jaws felt like iron;
she was shaking with fury.

Then she saw the bear. It was not twenty meters
away.

"Quiet!" she hissed. They went on talking loudly.

"QUIET!" she shouted, and as the talk died down to
an injured and peevish mutter, she saw that the bear—
if it was a bear—had heard them and was slowly, curiously, calmly, coming over to investigate. It seemed to
be grayish-white, like the snow, and longer in the neck
than it should be.

"Don't move," she said very softly, "there is an animal
out here," and in the silence that followed she saw the
creature hesitate, swaying a little or lumbering from side
to side. It might very well pass them by. It stopped,
sniffed about and stood there for what seemed three or
four minutes, then fell clumsily on to all fours and began
to move slowly away.

Then Maudey screamed. Undecided no longer, the
animal turned and flowed swiftly towards them, unbelievably graceful over the broken ground and the sharply
sloping hillside. Alyx stood very still. She said, "Machine, your bow," and heard Gunnar whisper "Kill it,
kill it, why don't you kill it!" The beast was almost upon
her. At the last moment she knelt and sent a bolt between its eyes; then she dropped down automatically

and swiftly, rolling to one side, dropping the bow. She snatched her knives from both her sleeves and threw herself under the swaying animal, driving up between the ribs first with one hand and then the other. The thing fell on her immediately like a dead weight; it was too enormous, too heavy for her to move; she lay there trying to breathe, slowly blacking out and feeling her ribs begin to give way. Then she fainted and came to to find Gunnar and Machine rolling the enormous carcass off her. She lay, a swarm of black sparks in front of her eyes. Machine wiped the beast's blood off her suit—it came off absolutely clean with a handful of snow—and carried her like a doll to a patch of clean snow where she began to breathe. The blood rushed back to her head. She could think again.

"It's dead," said Gunnar unsteadily, "I think it died at once from the bolt."

"Oh you devils!" gasped Alyx.

"*I* came out at once," said Machine, with some relish. "He didn't." He began pressing his hands rhythmically against her sides. She felt better.

"The boy—the boy put a second bolt in it," said Gunnar, after a moment's hesitation. "I was afraid," he added. "I'm sorry."

"Who let that woman scream?" said Alyx.

Gunnar shrugged helplessly.

"Always know anatomy," said Machine, with astonishing cheerfulness. "You see, the human body is a machine. I know some things," and he began to drag the animal away.

"Wait," said Alyx. She found she could walk. She went over and looked at the thing. It was a bear but like none she had ever seen or heard of: a white bear with a long, snaky neck, almost four meters high if it had chosen to stand. The fur was very thick.

"It's a polar bear," said Gunnar.

She wanted to know what that was.

"It's an Old Earth animal," he said, "but it must have been adapted. They usually live in the sea, I think. They have been stocking Paradise with Old Earth animals. I thought you knew."

"*I did not know*," said Alyx.

"I'm—I'm sorry," he said, "but I never—never thought of it. I didn't think it would matter." He looked down at the enormous corpse. "Animals do not attack people," he said. Even in the dim light she could see his expression; he knew that what he had said was idiotic.

"Oh no," she said deliberately, "oh no, of course not," and kneeling beside the corpse she extracted both her knives, cleaned them in the snow and put them back in the sheaths attached to her forearms under the suit. Convenient not to have water rust the blades. She studied the bear's claws for a few minutes, feeling them and trying as well as she could to see them in the dim light. Then she sent Machine into the cave for Raydos's artists' tools, and choosing the small, thin knife that he used to sharpen his pencils (some day, she thought, she would have to ask him what a pencils was) she slashed the animal's belly and neck, imitating the slash of claws and disguising the wounds made by her knives. She

61

had seen bears fight once, in a circus, and had heard tales of what they did to one another. She hoped the stories had been accurate. With Raydos's knife she also ripped open one of the animal's shoulders and attempted to simulate the bite of its teeth, being careful to open a main artery. The damned thing had such a layer of fat that she had trouble getting to it. When cut, the vessel pumped slowly; there was not the pool of blood there should be, but *What the devil,* she thought, *no one may ever find it and if they do, will they be able to tell the difference? Probably not.* They could dig out the bolts tomorrow. She cleaned Raydos's knife, returned it to Machine and went back to the cave.

No one said a word.

"I have," said Alyx, "just killed a bear. It was eleven feet high and could have eaten the lot of you. If anyone talks loud again, any time, for any reason, I shall ram his unspeakable teeth down his unspeakable throat."

Maudey began to mutter, sobbing a little.

"Machine," she said, "make that woman stop," and she watched, dead tired, while Machine took something from his pack, pressed it to Maudey's nose, and laid her gently on the floor. "She'll sleep," he said.

"That was not kindly done," remarked one of the nuns.

Alyx bit her own hand; she bit it hard, leaving marks; she told Machine, Raydos and Gunnar about the watch; she and they brought more snow into the cave to cushion the others, although the wind had half done their job for them. Everyone was quiet. All the same, she put her fingers in her ears but that pushed her hood back and made her head get cold; then she rolled over against the cave wall. Finally she did what she had been doing for the past seventeen nights. She went out into the snow and slept by herself, against the rock wall two meters from the drop, with Machine nearby, dim and comforting in the falling snow. She dreamed of the sun of the Tyrian seas, of clouds and ships and Mediterranean heat—and then of nothing at all.

The next morning when the East—she had decided to call it the East—brightened enough to see by, Alyx ended her watch. It had begun to clear during the night and the sky was showing signs of turning a pale winter blue, very uncomfortable-looking. She woke Gunnar, making the others huddled near him stir and mutter in their sleep, for it had gotten colder, too, during the night, and with Gunnar she sat down in the snow and went over the contents of their two packs, item by item. She figured that what they had in common everyone would have. She made him explain everything: the sun-glasses, the drugs that slowed you down if you were hurt, the bottle Machine had used that was for unconsciousness in cases of pain, the different kinds of dried foods, the binoculars, a bottle of something you put on wounds to make new flesh (it said "nu-flesh" and she tried to memorize the letters on it), the knives, the grooved barrel of the crossbow (but that impressed her

63

greatly), the water containers, the suit-mending tape, fluff you could add to your suit if you lost fluff from it and a coil of extremely thin, extremely strong rope that she measured by solemnly telling it out from her outstretched hand to her nose and so on and so on and so on until she had figured the length. Gunnar seemed to find this very funny. There was also something that she recognized as long underwear (though she did not think she would bring it to anybody's attention just yet) and at the bottom a packet of something she could not make head or tail of; Gunnar said it was to unfold and clean yourself with.

"Everyone's used theirs up," said he, "I'm afraid."

"A ritual, no doubt," said she, "in this cold. I told them they'd stink."

He sat there, wrinkling his brow for a moment, and then he said:

"There are no stimulants and there are no euphorics."

She asked what those were and he explained. "Ah, a Greek root," she said. He started to talk about how worried he was that there were no stimulants and no euphorics; these should have been included; they could hardly expect them to finish a weekend without them, let alone a seven-weeks' trip; in fact, he said, there was something odd about the whole thing. By now Alyx had ambled over to the dead bear and was digging the bolts out of it; she asked him over her shoulder, "Do *they* travel by night or day?"

"They?" he said, puzzled, and then "Oh, them! No, it makes no difference to them."

"Then it will make no difference to us," she said, cleaning the bolts in the snow. "Can they follow our tracks at night?"

"Why not?" said he, and she nodded.

"Do you think," said he, after a moment's silence, "that they are trying something out on us?"

"They?" she said. "Oh, them! Trans-Temp. Possibly. Quite possibly." *But probably not,* she added to herself, *unfortunately.* And she packed the bolts neatly away.

"*I* think," said Gunnar, skirting the bear's carcass where the blood still showed under the trodden snow, "that it is very odd that we have nothing else with us. I'm inclined to—" (*Good Lord, he's nervous,* she thought) "I'm inclined to believe," he said, settling ponderously in a clean patch of snow and leaning towards her so as to make himself heard, for he was speaking in a low voice, "that this is some kind of experiment. Or carelessness. Criminal carelessness. When we get back—" and he stopped, staring into the snow.

"If we get back," said Alyx cheerfully, getting to her feet, "you can lodge a complaint or declare a tort, or whatever it is you do. Here," and she handed him a wad of fluff she had picked out of her pack.

"What I should have done last night," she said, "half-obliterating our tracks around the carcass so they don't look so damned human. With luck" (she glanced up) "the snow won't stop for an hour yet."

"How can you tell?" said he, his mouth open.

"Because it is still coming down," said Alyx, and she gave him a push in the back. She had to reach up to do it. He bent and the two of them backed away, drawing the wads of fluff across the snow like brooms. It worked, but not well.

"How about those nuns," said Alyx. "Don't they have some damned thing or other with them?"

"Oh, you have to be careful!" he said in a whisper. "You have to be careful about *that!*" and with this he worked his way to the mouth of the cave.

The sleepers were coming out.

Waking up by themselves for the first time, they filed out of the cave and stood in a row in the opening staring down at the corpse of the animal they had not even seen the night before. She suspected the story had gotten around. *Twenty hand-spans,* she thought, *of bear.* The nuns started back, making some kind of complicated sign on their foreheads and breasts. Raydos bowed admiringly, half ironically. The two older people were plainly frightened, even though Maudey had begun to crane forward for a better look; suddenly her whole body jerked and she flung out one arm; she would have overbalanced herself and fallen if Gavrily had not caught her. "After-effects," he said.

"How long do these go on?" said Alyx, a little wearily.

"A couple of days," he said quickly, holding on to the frightened woman, "only a couple of days. They get better."

"Then take care of her until they do," said Alyx, and she was about to add the usual signal for the morning (COME ON!) when a voice somewhere above her head said:

66

"Agent?"

It was Iris, that great lolloping girl, almost as high as the bear, looking down at her with the unfathomable expression of the very young, twisting and twisting a lock of silver hair that had escaped from her hood. She was really very pretty.

"Agent," blurted Iris, her eyes big, "will you teach me how to shoot?"

"Yes, my dear," said Alyx, "indeed I will."

"Come on!" she bawled then. They came on.

Later in the morning, when she allowed them to stop and eat the soggiest of their protein and dried starch kernels for breakfast, one of the nuns came up to her, squatted gracefully in the snow and made the complicated sign thrice: once on her own forehead, once on her own breast and once in the air between her and the little woman who had shot the bear.

"Violence," said the nun earnestly, "is deplorable. It is always deplorable. It corrupts love, you see, and love is the expansion of consciousness while violence is the restriction of love so that violence, which restricts love and consciousness, is always bad, as consciousness is always good and the consciousness of the All is the best and only good, and to restrict what may lead to the consciousness of the All is unwise and unkind. Therefore to die is only to merge with the All so that actually violence is not justifiable in the postponing of death, as we must all die, and dying is the final good if it is a dying into the All and not a dying away from it, as in violence."

"But," she said, "the recognition of consciousness and the value of expression of consciousness go hand in hand; there is no evil in expressing the impulses of the nature of consciousness, so that there can be no evil in action and action is not violence. Action is actually an expansion of the consciousness, as one becomes more aware of one's particular true nature and thence slowly more aware of one's ultimate all-embracing Nature which unites one with the All. Action is therefore a good. It is not, of course, the same thing as the true religion, but some of us go the slow path and some the quick, and who will attain Enlightenment first? Who knows? What is, is, as the sage said: One way is not another. I hope you will attend our services when we return home."

"Yes," said Alyx. "Indeed I will." The tall lady made the sign again, this time on Alyx's forehead and breast, and went sedately back to her breakfast.

And that, thought Alyx, *is the damndest way of saying Bravo that I have ever heard!*

She decided to teach them all to shoot, including the nuns. It was understood, of course, that the nuns would shoot only bears.

Later in the afternoon, when the snow had stopped and before visibility became bad, she lined all of them up on a relatively level snow-field, assigning the two nuns to Gunnar, Gavrily and Raydos to Machine and herself teaching Iris. Maudey rested, a little dazed from the nervous spasms that had been shaking her all day, though perfectly clear in her mind. Most of them tired of the business after the first hour, except for Raydos, who seemed to enjoy handling the new thing again, and Iris, who kept saying "Just a little more, just a little more; I'm not good enough." When Machine laughed at her, she loftily explained that it was "rather like dancing."

"Which you have never done for pleasure, I am sure," she added.

During the late afternoon they slogged up an ever-narrowing path between cliffs, towards what Gunnar swore was a pass in the mountains. It seemed, however, as if these mountains had no pass but only plateaus; no, not plateaus, only peaks; that even the peaks had no down but only up, and on and on they kept in the red light of the setting winter sun, holding the glare always to the proper side of them, plodding up a steeper and steeper path until the red light turned purple and dim, and died, until each of them saw the other as a dim hulk marching in front of him.

She called a halt. They sat down. For the first time during the whole trip they bunched together, actually touching body to body, with only Maudey a little away from them, for she was still having her trouble. (Alyx had one of the nuns put her to sleep and the spasms stopped instantly.) It was very cold, with the stars splendid, icy points and the whole tumbled waste of jagged rock shining faintly around them. They did not, as they usually did, begin to analyze the events of the day, but only half-sat, half-lay in silence, feeling the still air around them drain away their warmth, which (Iris said) "seemed to flow right up into the sky." They watched the stars. Then out of nowhere, for no reason at all, Gavrily began to sing in a reedy tenor a few lines of what he called a "baby-song" and this nursery tune—for it was not, Alyx was made to understand, real music—put them all into tears. They sobbed companionably for a little while. It got colder and colder. Gunnar suggested that they pack the snow around them to keep in the heat and Alyx, who had noticed that her buttocks seemed to be the warmest place about her, agreed, so they all built a round wall of snow, with Maudey in the middle of it, and then crawled in around her and pulled the whole thing down on top of them, each packing himself in his own little heap. Then it all had to be disrupted and put right again because the first watch had to climb out. This was Iris. She still seemed very excited, whispering to Alyx "Was I good enough? Will you teach me again?" over and over until somebody poked her and she exclaimed "Ow!" There was yawning, sighing, breathing.

"Will you," said Iris, bending over the little heap of persons, "teach me again? Will you tell me all about yourself? Will you tell me everything? Will you? Will you?"

"Oh, be quiet," said Machine crossly, and Iris took her bow and went a little aside, to sit watch.

It was the eighteenth night.

The nineteenth. The twentieth. The twenty-first. They were very quiet. They were idealizing, trusting, companionable, almost happy. It made Alyx nervous, and the more they looked at her, asked her about her and listened to her the more unnerved she became. She did not think they understood what was happening. She told them about her life with one ear on the sounds about them, instantly alert, ready to spring up, with her crossbow always across her knees; so that they asked her what the matter was. She said "Nothing." She told them legends, fairy tales, religious stories, but they didn't want to hear those; they wanted to hear about her; what she ate, what she drank, what she wore, what her house was like, whom she knew, all the particulars of the business, the alleyways, the gutters, the finest houses and the worst houses in Tyre. She felt it was all being dragged out of her against her will. They were among the mountains now and going very slowly, very badly; they went far into the night now whenever it was clear and as soon as they settled down for the night (everyone had got into the long underwear one clear and frosty morning, hopping about from one bare foot to another, and discovering wrapped within it what they declared to be artificial arches) they bunched up together against the cold, interlacing arms and legs and squirming together as close as they could, saying:

"Tell us about—"

She told them.

On the twenty-fourth night, when she woke Machine to take the dawn watch, he said to her "Do you want to climb it?"

"Climb what?" muttered Alyx. She was chilled and uncomfortable, stirring around to get her blood up.

"Do you want to climb it?" said Machine patiently.

"Wait a minute," she said, "let me think." Then she said "You'd better not use slang; I don't think I'm programmed for it."

He translated. He added—off-handedly—"You don't have to worry about pregnancy; Trans-Temp's taken care of it. Or they will, when we get back."

"Well, no," said Alyx. "No, I don't think I do want to —climb it." He looked, as far as she could tell in the dim light, a little surprised; but he did not touch her, he did not ask again or laugh or stir or even move. He sat with his arms around his knees as if considering something and then he said "All right." He repeated it decisively, staring at her with eyes that were just beginning to turn blue with the dawn; then he smiled, pulled back the spring on his crossbow and got to his feet.

"And keep your eyes open," she said, on her way back to the snow-heaped nest of the others.

"Don't I always?" he said, and as she turned away she heard an unmistakable sound. He had laughed.

The next day Raydos started to sketch her at every halt. He took out his materials and worked swiftly but easily, like a man who thinks himself safe. It was intolerable. She told him that if anything happened or anyone came he would either have to drop his sketchbook or put it in his pack; that if he took the time to put it into his pack he might die or betray the lot of them and that if he dropped it, someone might find it.

"They won't know what it is," he said. "It's archaic, you see."

"They'll know it's not an animal," she said. "Put it away."

He went on sketching. She walked over to him, took the book of papers and the length of black thing he was using away from him and stowed them away in her own pack. He smiled and blinked in the sunlight. The thing was not real charcoal or gum or even chalky; she considered asking him about it and then she shuddered. She stood there for a moment, shading her eyes against the sun and being frightened, as if she had to be frightened for the whole crew of them as well as herself, as if she were alone, more alone than by herself, and the more they liked her, the more they obeyed, the more they talked of "when we get back," the more frightened she would have to become.

"All right, come on," she heard herself say.

"All right, come on."

"Come on!"

Time after time after time.

On the twenty-ninth afternoon Maudey died. She died suddenly and by accident. They were into the pass that Gunnar had spoken of, half blinded by the glare of ice on the rock walls to either side, following a path that dropped almost sheer from the left. It was wide enough for two or three and Machine had charge of Maudey that day, for although her nervous fits had grown less frequent, they had never entirely gone away. He walked on the outside, she on the inside. Behind them Iris was humming softly to herself. It was icy in parts and the going was slow. They stopped for a moment and Machine cautiously let go of Maudey's arm; at the same time Iris began to sing softly, the same drab tune over and over again, the way she had said to Alyx they danced at the drug palaces, over and over to put themselves into trances, over and over.

"Stop that filthy song," said Maudey. "I'm tired."

Iris continued insultingly to sing.

"I'm tired!" said Maudey desperately, "I'm tired! I'm tired!" and in turning she slipped and fell on the slippery path to her knees. She was still in balance, however. Iris had arched her eyebrows and was silently mouthing something when Machine, who had been watching Maudey intently, bent down to take hold of her, but at that instant Maudey's whole right arm threw itself out over nothing and she fell over the side of the path. Machine flung himself after her and was only stopped from falling over in his turn by fetching up against someone's foot—it happened to be one of the nuns—and they both went down, teetering for a moment over the side. The nun was sprawled on the path in a patch of gravel and Machine hung shoulders down over the verge. They pulled him back and got the other one to her feet.

"Well, what happened?" said Iris in surprise. Alyx had grabbed Gunnar by the arm. Iris shrugged at them

74

all elaborately and sat down, her chin on her knees, while Alyx got the rope from all the packs as swiftly as possible, knotted it, pushed the nun off the patch of dry gravel and set Machine on it. "Can you hold him?" she said. Machine nodded. She looped the rope about a projecting point in the wall above them and gave it to Machine; the other end she knotted under Gunnar's arms. They sent him down to bring Maudey up, which he did, and they laid her down on the path. She was dead.

"Well, how is she?" said Iris, looking at them all over her shoulder.

"She's dead," said Alyx.

"That," said Iris brightly, "is not the right answer," and she came over to inspect things for herself, coquettishly twisting and untwisting a lock of her straight silver hair. She knelt by the body. Maudey's head lay almost flat against her shoulder for her neck was broken; her eyes were wide open. Alyx closed them, saying again "Little girl, she's dead." Iris looked away, then up at them, then down again. She made a careless face. She said "Mo—Maudey was old, you know; d'you think they can fix her when we get back?"

"She is dead," said Alyx. Iris was drawing lines in the snow. She shrugged and looked covertly at the body, then she turned to it and her face began to change; she moved nearer on her knees. "Mo—Mother," she said, then grabbed at the woman with the funny, twisted neck, screaming the word "Mother" over and over, grabbing at the clothing and the limbs and even the purple hair where the hood had fallen back, screaming without stopping. Machine said quickly, "I can put her out." Alyx shook her head. She put one hand over Iris's mouth to muffle the noise. She sat with the great big girl as Iris threw herself on top of dead Maudey, trying to burrow into her, her screaming turning to sobbing, great gasping sobs that seemed to dislocate her whole body, just as vanity and age had thrown her mother about so terribly between them and had finally thrown her over a cliff. As soon as the girl began to cry, Alyx put both arms about her and rocked with her, back and forth. One of the nuns came up with a thing in her hand, a white pill.

"It would be unkind," said the nun, "it would be most unkind, most unkind—"

"Go to hell," said Alyx in Greek.

"I must insist," said the nun softly, "I must, must insist," in a tangle of hisses like a snake. "I must, must, I must—"

"Get out!" shouted Alyx to the startled woman, who did not even understand the words. With her arms around Iris, big as Iris was, with little Iris in agonies, Alyx talked to her in Greek, soothed her in Greek, talked just to be talking, rocked her back and forth. Finally there came a moment when Iris stopped.

Everyone looked very surprised.

"Your mother," said Alyx, carefully pointing to the body, "is dead." This provoked a fresh outburst. Three more times. Four times. Alyx said it again. For several hours she repeated the whole thing, she did not know how often, holding the girl each time, then holding only her hand, then finally drawing her to her feet and away from the dead woman while the men took the food and equipment out of Maudey's pack to divide it among themselves and threw the body over the path, to hide it. There was a kind of tittering, whispering chatter behind Alyx. She walked all day with the girl, talking to her, arm clumsily about her, making her walk while she shook with fits of weeping, making her walk when she wanted to sit down, making her walk as she talked of her mother, of running away from home—"not like you did" said Iris—of hating her, loving her, hating her, being reasonable, being rational, being grown up, fighting ("but it's natural!"), not being able to stand her, being able to stand her, loving her, always fighting with her (and here a fresh fit of weeping) and then—then—

"I killed her!" cried Iris, stock-still on the path. "Oh my God, I killed her! I! I!"

"Bullshit," said Alyx shortly, her hypnotic vocabulary coming to the rescue at the eleventh instant.

"But I did, I did," said Iris. "Didn't you see? I upset her, I made—"

"Ass!" said Alyx.

"Then why didn't you rope them together," cried Iris, planting herself hysterically in front of Alyx, arms akimbo, "why didn't you? You knew she could fall! You wanted to kill her!"

"If you say that again—" said Alyx, getting ready.

"I see it, I see it," whispered Iris wildly, putting her

arms around herself, her eyes narrowing. "Yesss, you wanted her dead—you didn't want the *trouble*—"

Alyx hit her across the face. She threw her down, sat on her and proceeded to pound at her while the others watched, shocked and scandalized. She took good care not to hurt her. When Iris had stopped, she rubbed snow roughly over the girl's face and hauled her to her feet, "and no more trouble out of you!" she said.

"I'm all right," said Iris uncertainly. She took a step. "Yes," she said. Alyx did not hold her any more but walked next to her, giving her a slight touch now and then when she seemed to waver.

"Yes, I am all right," said Iris. Then she added, in her normal voice, "I know Maudey is dead."

"Yes," said Alyx.

"I know," said Iris, her voice wobbling a little, "that you didn't put them together because they both would have gone over."

She added, "I am going to cry."

"Cry away," said Alyx, and the rest of the afternoon Iris marched steadily ahead, weeping silently, trying to mop her face and her nose with the cleaning cloth Alyx had given her, breaking out now and again into suppressed, racking sobs. They camped for the night in a kind of hollow between two rising slopes with Iris jammed securely into the middle of everybody and Alyx next to her. In the dim never-dark of the snow fields, long after everyone else had fallen asleep, someone brushed Alyx across the face, an oddly unctuous sort of touch, at once gentle and unpleasant. She knew at once who it was.

"If you do not," she said, "take that devil's stuff out of here *at once—!*" The hand withdrew.

"I must insist," said the familiar whisper, "I must, must insist. You do not understand—it is not—"

"If you touch her," said Alyx between her teeth, "I will kill you—both of you—and I will take those little pills you are so fond of and defecate upon each and every one of them, upon my soul I swear that I will!"

"But—but—" She could feel the woman trembling with shock.

"If you so much as touch her," said Alyx, "you will have caused me to commit two murders and a sacrilege. Now get out!" and she got up in the dim light, pulled the pack off every grunting, protesting sleeper's back—except the two women who had withdrawn to a little distance together—and piled them like a barricade around Iris, who was sleeping with her face to the stars and her mouth open. *Let them trip over that,* she thought vindictively. *Damn it! Damn them all! Boots without spikes, damn them! What do they expect us to do, swim over the mountains?* She did not sleep for a long time, and when she did it seemed that everyone was climbing over her, stepping on top of her and sliding off just for fun. She dreamed she was what Gunnar had described as a ski-slide. Then she dreamed that the first stepped on to her back and then the second on to his and so on and so on until they formed a human ladder, when the whole snow-field slowly tilted upside down. Everyone fell off. She came to with a start; it was Gavrily, waking her for the dawn watch. She saw him fall asleep in seconds, then trudged a little aside and sat cross-legged, her bow on her knees. The two nuns had moved back to the group, asleep, sprawled out and breathing softly with the others. She watched the sky lighten to the left, become transparent, take on color. Pale blue. Winter blue.

"All right," she said, "everyone up!" and slipped off her pack for the usual handfuls of breakfast food.

The first thing she noticed, with exasperation, was that Raydos had stolen back his art equipment, for it was gone. The second was that there were only six figures sitting up and munching out of their cupped hands, not seven; she thought *that's right, Maudey's dead*, then ran them over in her head: *Gunnar, Gavrily, Raydos, Machine, the Twins, Iris—*

But Iris was missing.

Her first thought was that the girl had somehow been spirited away, or made to disappear by The Holy Twins, who had stopped eating with their hands halfway to their mouths, like people about to pour a sacrifice of grain on to the ground for Mother Earth. Both of them were watching her. Her second thought was unprintable and almost—but not quite—unspeakable, and so instantaneous that she had leapt into the circle of breakfasters before she half knew where she was, shoving their packs and themselves out of her way. She dislodged one of Raydos's eye lenses; he clapped his hand to his eye and began to grope in the snow. "What the devil—!" said Gunnar.

Iris was lying on her back among the packs, looking up into the sky. She had shut one eye and the other was moving up and down in a regular pattern. Alyx fell over her. When she scrambled to her knees, Iris had not moved and her one open eye still made the regular transit of nothing, up and down, up and down.

"Iris," said Alyx.

"Byootiful," said Iris. Alyx shook her. "Byootiful," crooned the girl, "all byootiful" and very slowly she opened her closed eye, shut the other and began again to scan the something or nothing up in the sky, up and down, up and down. Alyx tried to pull the big girl to her feet, but she was too heavy; then with astonishing lightness Iris herself sat up, put her head to one side and looked at Alyx with absolute calm and complete relaxation. It seemed to Alyx that the touch of one finger would send her down on her back again. "Mother," said Iris clearly, opening both eyes, "mother. Too lovely," and she continued to look at Alyx as she had at the sky. She bent her head down on to one shoulder, as Maudey's head had been bent in death with a broken neck.

"Mother is lovely," said Iris conversationally. "There she is. You are lovely. Here you are. He is lovely. There he is. She is lovely. We are lovely. They are lovely. I am lovely. Love is lovely. Lovely lovely lovely lovely —" she went on talking to herself as Alyx stood up. One of the nuns came walking across the trampled snow with her hands clasped nervously in front of her; she came up to the little woman and took a breath; then she said:

"You may kill me if you like."

"I love shoes," said Iris, lying down on her back, "I love sky. I love clouds. I love hair. I love zippers. I love food. I love my mother. I love feet. I love bathrooms. I love walking. I love people. I love sleep. I love breathing. I love tape. I love books. I love pictures. I love air. I love rolls. I love hands. I love—"

"Shut up!" shouted Alyx, as the girl continued with her inexhaustible catalogue. "Shut up, for God's sake!" and turned away, only to find herself looking up at the face of the nun, who had quickly moved about to be in front of her and who still repeated, "You may kill us both if you like," with an unbearable mixture of nervousness and superiority. Iris had begun to repeat the word "love" over and over and over again in a soft, unchanging voice.

"Is this not kinder?" said the nun.

"Go away before I kill you!" said Alyx.

"She is happy," said the nun.

"She is an idiot!"

"She will be happy for a day," said the nun, "and then less happy and then even less happy, but she will have her memory of the All and when the sadness comes back—as it will in a day or so, I am sorry to say, but some day we will find out how—"

"Get out!" said Alyx.

"However, it will be an altered sadness," continued

the nun rapidly, "an eased sadness with the All in its infinite All—"

"Get out of here before I alter *you* into the All!" Alyx shouted, losing control of herself. The nun hurried away and Alyx, clapping both hands over her ears, walked rapidly away from Iris, who had begun to say "*I've* been to the moon but *you* won't. *I've* been to the sun but *you* won't, *I've* been to—" and over and over and over again with ascending and descending variations.

"Messing up the machinery," said Machine, next to her.

"Leave me alone," said Alyx, her hands still over her ears. The ground had unaccountably jumped up and was swimming in front of her; she knew she was crying.

"I don't approve of messing up the machinery," said Machine softly. "I have a respect for the machinery; I do not like to see it abused and if they touch the girl again you need not kill them. I will."

"No killing," said Alyx, as levelly as she could.

"Religion?" said Machine sarcastically.

"No," said Alyx, lifting her head abruptly, "but no killing. Not my people." She turned to go, but he caught her gently by the arm, looking into her face with a half-mocking smile, conveying somehow by his touch that her arm was not inside an insulated suit but was bare, and that he was stroking it. The trip had given him back his eyebrows and eyelashes; the hair on his head was a wiry black brush; for Machine did not, apparently, believe in tampering irreversibly with the Machinery. She thought *I won't get involved with any of these peo-*

ple. She found herself saying idiotically "Your hair's growing in." He smiled and took her other arm, holding her as if he were going to lift her off the ground, she hotter and dizzier every moment, feeling little, feeling light, feeling like a woman who has had no luxury for a long, long time. She said, "Put me down, if you please."

"Tiny," he said, "you *are* down," and putting his hands around her waist, he lifted her easily to the height of his face. "I think you will climb it," he said.

"No," said Alyx. It did not seem to bother him to keep holding her up in the air.

"I think you will," he said, smiling, and still smiling, he kissed her with a sort of dispassionate, calm pleasure, taking his time, holding her closely and carefully, using the thoughtful, practiced, craftsmanly thoroughness that Machine brought to everything that Machine did. Then he put her down and simply walked away.

"Ah, go find someone your own size!" she called after him, but then she remembered that the only girl his size was Iris, and that Iris was lying on her back in the snow in a world where everything was lovely, lovely, lovely due to a little white pill. She swore. She could see Iris in the distance, still talking. She took a knife out of her sleeve and tried the feel of it but the feel was wrong, just as the boots attached to their suits had no spikes, just as their maps stopped at Base B, just as Paradise itself had turned into—but no, that was not so. The place was all right, quite all right. *The place,* she thought, *is all right.* She started back to the group of picnickers who were slipping their packs back on and

84

stamping the snow off their boots; some were dusting off the rear ends of others where they had sat in the snow. She saw one of The Heavenly Twins say something in Iris's ear and Iris get obediently to her feet, still talking; then the other nun said something and Iris's mouth stopped moving.

Bury it deep, thought Alyx, *never let it heal*. She joined them, feeling like a mule-driver.

"D'you know," said Gunnar conversationally, "that we've been out here thirty days? Not bad, eh?"

"I'll say!" said Gavrily.

"And only one death," said Alyx sharply, "not bad, eh?"

"That's not our fault," said Gavrily. They were all staring at her.

"No," she said, "it's not our fault. It's mine.

"Come on," she added.

On the thirty-second day Paradise still offered them the semblance of a path, though Gunnar could not find his mountain pass and grew scared and irritable trying to lead them another way. Paradise tilted and zigzagged around them. At times they had to sit down, or slide down, or even crawl, and he waited for them with deep impatience, telling them haughtily how a professional would be able to handle this sort of thing without getting down on his———to go down a slope. Alyx said nothing. Iris spoke to nobody. Only Gavrily talked incessantly about People's Capitalism, as if he

had been stung by a bug, explaining at great and unnecessary length how the Government was a check on
the Military, the Military was a check on Government,
and both were a check on Business which in turn checked
the other two. He called it the three-part system of
checks and balances. Alyx listened politely. Finally she
said:

"What's a————?"

Gavrily explained, disapprovingly.

"Ah," said Alyx, smiling.

Iris still said nothing.

They camped early for the night, sprawled about a
narrow sort of table-land, as far away from each other
as they could get and complaining loudly. The sun had
not been down for fifteen minutes and there was still
light in the sky: rose, lavender, yellow, apple-green,
violet. It made a beautiful show. It was getting extremely cold. Gunnar insisted that they could go on, in
spite of their complaints; he clenched his big hands and
ordered them to get up (which they did not do); then
he turned to Alyx.

"You too," he said. "You can go on for another hour."

"I'd prefer not to go on in the dark," she said. She
was lying down with her hands under her head, watching the colors in the sky.

"There's light enough to last us all night!" he said.
"Will you come on?"

"No," said Alyx.

"God damn it!" he said, "do you think I don't know

86

what I'm doing? Do you think I don't know where I'm taking you? You lazy sons of bitches, get up!"

"That's enough," said Alyx, half on her feet.

"Oh no it isn't," he said. "Oh no it isn't! You all get up, all of you! You're not going to waste the hour that's left!"

"I prefer," said Alyx quietly, "not to sleep with my head wedged in a chasm, if you don't mind." She rose to her feet.

"Do I have to kick you in the stomach again?" she said calmly.

Gunnar was silent. He stood with his hands balled into fists.

"Do I?" she said. "Do I have to kick you in the groin? Do I have to gouge your eyes out?"

"Do I have to dive between your legs and throw you head foremost on the rocks so you're knocked out?" she said.

"So your nose gets broken?"

"So your cheekbones get bloody and your chin bruised?"

She turned to the others.

"I suggest that we keep together," she said, "to take advantage of each other's warmth; otherwise you are bound to stiffen up as you get colder; it is going to be a devil of a night."

She joined the others as they packed snow about themselves—it was more like frozen dust than snow, and there was not much of it; they were too high up— and settled in against Iris, who was unreadable, with

87

the beautiful sky above them dying into deep rose, into dusty rose, into dirty rose. She did not look at Gunnar. She felt sorry for him. He was to take the first watch anyway, *though* (she thought) *what we are watching for I do not know and what we could do if we saw it, God only knows. And then what I am watching for . . . What I would do . . . No food . . . Too high up . . . No good . . .*

She woke under the night sky, which was brilliant with stars: enormous, shining, empty and cold. The stars were unrecognizable, not constellations she knew any more but planes upon planes, shifting trapezoids, tilted pyramids like the mountains themselves, all reaching off into spaces she could not even begin to comprehend: distant suns upon suns. The air was very cold.

Someone was gently shaking her, moving her limbs, trying to untangle her from the mass of human bodies. She said, "Lemme sleep" and tried to turn over. Then she felt a shocking draught at her neck and breast and a hand inside her suit; she said sleepily, "Oh dear, it's too cold."

"You had better get up," whispered Machine reasonably. "I believe I'm standing on somebody.

"I'm trying not to," he added solemnly, "but everyone's so close together that it's rather difficult."

Alyx giggled. The sound startled her. *Well, I'll talk to you,* she said. *No,* she thought, *I didn't say it, did I?* She articulated clearly "I—will—talk—to you," and sat up, leaning her head against his knee to wake up. She pushed his hand away and closed up her suit. "I'm cross," she said, "you hear that?"

"I hear and obey," whispered Machine, grinning, and taking her up in his arms like a baby, he carried her through the mass of sleepers, picking his way carefully, for they were indeed packed very close together. He set her down a little distance away.

"You're supposed to be on watch," she protested. He shook his head. He knelt beside her and pointed to the watch—Gunnar—some fifteen meters away. *A noble figure*, thought Alyx. She began to laugh uncontrollably, muffling her mouth on her knees. Machine's shoulders were shaking gleefully. He scooped her up with one arm and walked her behind a little wall of snow someone had built, a little wall about one meter high and three meters long—

"Did you—?" said Alyx.

"I did," said the young man. He reached out with one forefinger and rapidly slid it down the opening of her suit from her neck to her—

"Eeeey, it's too cold!" cried Alyx, rolling away and pressing the opening shut again.

"Sssh!" he said. "No it's not."

"He'll see us," said Alyx, straightening out distrustfully.

"No he won't."

"Yes he will."

"No he won't."

"Yes he *will!*" and she got up, shook the snow off herself and immediately started away. Machine did not move.

"Well, aren't you—" she said, nettled.

He shook his head. He sat down, crossed his legs in some unaccountable fashion so the feet ended up on top, crossed his arms, and sat immobile as an Oriental statue. She came back and sat next to him, resting her head against him (as much as she could with one of his knees in the way), feeling soulful, trustful, silly. She could feel him chuckling. "How *do* you do that with the feet?" she said. He wriggled his toes inside his boots.

"I dare not do anything else," he said, "because of your deadly abilities with groin-kicking, eye-gouging, head-cracking and the like, Agent."

"Oh, shut up!" said Alyx. She put her arms around him. He uncrossed his own arms, then used them to carefully uncross his legs; then lay down with her in the snow, insulated suit to insulated suit, kissing her time after time. Then he stopped.

"You're scared, aren't you?" he whispered.

She nodded.

"Goddammit, I've had men before!" she whispered. He put his finger over her lips. With the other hand he pressed together the ends of the thongs that could hold a suit loosely together at the collarbone—first his suit, then hers—and then, with the same hand, rapidly opened both suits from the neck in front to the base of the spine in back and ditto with the long underwear: "Ugly but useful," he remarked. Alyx began to giggle again. She tried to press against him, shivering with cold. "Wait!" he said, "and watch, O Agent," and very carefully, biting one lip, he pressed together the right-hand edges of both suits and then the left, making for the two of them a personal blanket, a double tent, a spot of warmth under the enormous starry sky.

"And they don't," he said triumphantly, "come apart by pulling. They *only* come apart by prying! And see? You can move your arms and legs in! Isn't it marvelous?" And he gave her a proud kiss—a big, delighted, impersonal smack on the cheek. Alyx began to laugh. She laughed as she pulled her arms and legs in to hug him; she laughed as he talked to her, as he buried his face in her neck, as he began to caress her; she laughed until her laughter turned to sobbing under his expert hands, his too-expert hands, his calm deliberateness; she raked his back with her fingernails; she screamed at him to hurry up and called him a pig and an actor and the son of a whore (for these epithets were of more or less equal value in her own country); and finally, when at his own good time the stars exploded—and she realized that *nova* meant—that *nova* meant (though she had closed her eyes a long time before)—someone had said *nova* the other day—she came to herself as if rocking in the shallows of a prodigious tide, yawning, lazily extending her toes—and with a vague but disquieting sense of having done something or said something she should not have said or done. She knew she hated him there, for a while; she was afraid she might have hurt him or hurt his feelings.

"What language were you speaking?" said Machine with interest.

"Greek!" said Alyx, and she laughed with relief and would have kissed him, only it was really too much effort.

He shook her. "Don't go to sleep," he said.

"Mmmm."

"Don't go to sleep!" and he shook her harder.

"Why not?" she said.

"Because," said Machine, "I am going to begin again."

"All right," said Alyx complaisantly and raised her knees. He began, as before, to kiss her neck, her shoulders and so on down et cetera et cetera, in short to do everything he had done before on the same schedule until it occurred to her that he was doing everything just as he had done it before and on the same schedule, until she tried to push him away, exclaiming angrily, feeling like a statuette or a picture, frightened and furious. At first he would not stop; finally she bit him.

"What the devil is the matter!" he cried.

"You," she said, "stop it. Let me out." They had been together and now they were sewed up in a sack; it was awful; she started to open the jointure of the suits but he grabbed her hands.

"What is it?" he said, "what is it? Don't you want it? Don't you see that I'm trying?"

"Trying?" said Alyx stupidly.

"Yes, trying!" he said vehemently. "Trying! Do you think that comes by nature?"

"I don't understand," she said. "I'm sorry." They lay silently for a few minutes.

"I was trying," he said in a thick, bitter voice, "to give you a good time. I like you. I did the best I could. Apparently it wasn't good enough."

"But I don't—" said Alyx.

"You don't want it," he said; "all right," and pushing her hands away, he began to open the suits himself. She closed them. He opened them and she closed them several times. Then he began to cry and she put her arms around him.

"I had the best time in my life," she said. He continued to sob, silently, through clenched teeth, turning away his face.

"I had," she repeated, "the best time in my life. I did. I did! But I don't want—"

"All right," he said.

"But I don't," she said, "I don't want—I don't—"

He tried to get away from her and, of course could not; he thrashed about, forgetting that the suits had to be slit and could not be pulled apart; he pushed against the material until he frightened her for she thought she was going to be hurt; finally she cried out:

"Darling, stop it! Please!"

Machine stopped, leaning on his knees and clenched fists, his face stubbornly turned away.

"It's you I want," she said. "D'you see? I don't want a—performance. I want *you*."

"I don't know what you're talking about," he said, more calmly.

"Well, I don't know what *you're* talking about," said Alyx reasonably.

"Look," he said, turning his head back so that they were nose to nose, "when you do something, you do it right, don't you?"

"No," said Alyx promptly.

"Well, what's the good of doing it then!" he shouted.

"Because you want to, idiot!" she snapped, "any five-year-old child—"

"Oh, now I'm a five-year-old child, am I?"

"Just a minute, just a minute, athlete! I never said—"

"Athlete! By God—"

She pinched him.

He pinched her.

She grabbed at what there was of his hair and pulled it; he howled and twisted her hand; then both of them pushed and the result was that he lost his balance and carried her over on to one side with him, the impromptu sleeping-bag obligingly going with them. They both got a faceful of snow. They wrestled silently for a few minutes, each trying to grab some part of the other, Machine muttering, Alyx kicking, Machine pushing her head down into the bag, Alyx trying to bite his finger, Machine yelling, Alyx trying to butt her head into his stomach. There was, however, no room to do anything properly. After a few minutes they stopped.

He sighed. It was rather peaceful, actually.

"Look, dear," he said quietly, "I've done my best. But if you want me, myself, you'll have to do without; I've heard that too often. Do you think they don't want me out there? Sure they do! They want me to open up my" (she could not catch the word) "like a God damned" (or that one) "and show them everything that's inside, all my feelings, or what they call feelings. I don't believe they have feelings. They talk about their complexities and their reactions and their impressions and their interactions and their patterns and their neuroses and their childhoods and their rebellions and their utterly unspeakable insides until I want to vomit. I have no insides. I will not have any. I certainly will not let anyone see any. I do things and I do them well; that's all. If you want that, you can have it. Otherwise, my love, I am simply not at home. Understood?"

"Understood," she said. She took his face in her hands. "You are splendid," she said thickly. "You are splendid and beautiful and superb. I love your performance. Perform me."

And if I let slip any emotion, she thought, *it will—thank God—be in Greek!*

He performed again—rather badly. But it turned out well just the same.

When Machine had gone to take over the watch from Gunnar, Alyx returned to the sleepers. Iris was sitting up. Not only was it possible to identify her face in the starlight reflected from the snow; she had thrown back her hood in the bitter cold and her silver hair glowed uncannily. She waited until Alyx reached her; then she said:

"Talk to me."

"Did you know I was up?" said Alyx. Iris giggled, but an uncertain, odd sort of giggle as if she were fighting for breath; she said in the same queer voice, "Yes, you woke me up. You were both shouting."

Gunnar must know, thought Alyx and dismissed the thought. She wondered if these people were jealous. She turned to go back to her own sleeping place but Iris clutched at her arm, repeating, "Talk to me!"

"What about, love?" said Alyx.

"Tell me—tell me bad things," said Iris, catching her breath and moving her head in the collar of her suit as if it were choking her. "Put your hood on," said Alyx, but the girl shook her head, declaring she wanted it that way. She said, "Tell me—horrors."

"What?" said Alyx in surprise, sitting down.

"I want to hear bad things," said Iris monotonously. "I want to hear awful things. I can't stand it. I keep slipping," and she giggled again, saying "Everybody could hear you all over camp," and then putting one hand to her face, catching her breath, and holding on to Alyx's arm as if she were drowning. "Tell me horrors!" she cried.

"Sssh," said Alyx, "ssssh, I'll tell you anything you like, baby, anything you like."

"My mother's dead," said Iris with sudden emotion. "My mother's dead. I've got to remember that. I've got to!"

"Yes, yes, she's dead," said Alyx.

"Please, please," said Iris, "keep me here. I keep sliding away."

"Horrors," said Alyx. "Good Lord, I don't think I know any tonight."

"It's like feathers," said Iris suddenly, dreamily, looking up in the sky, "it's like pillows, it's like air cushions under those things, you know, it's like—like—"

"All right, all right," said Alyx quickly, "your mother broke her neck. I'll tell you about it again. I might as well; you're all making me soft as wax, the whole lot of you."

"Don't, don't," said Iris, moaning. "Don't say soft. I keep trying, I thought the cold—yes, yes, that's good—" and with sudden decision she began to strip off her suit. Alyx grabbed her and wrestled her to the ground, fastening the suit again and shoving the hood on for good measure. She thought suddenly *She's still fighting the drug.* "You touch that again and I'll smash you," said Alyx steadily. "I'll beat your damned teeth in."

"It's too hot," said Iris feverishly, "too—to—" She relapsed into looking at the stars.

"Look at me," said Alyx, grabbing her head and pulling it down. "Look at me, baby."

"I'm not a baby," said Iris lazily. "I'm not a—a—baby. I'm a woman."

Alyx shook her.

"I am almost grown up," said Iris, not bothered by her head wobbling while she was being shaken. "I am very grown up. I am thirty-three."

Alyx dropped her hands.

"I am thirty-three already," continued Iris, trying to focus her eyes. "I am, I am" (she said this uncomfortably, with great concentration) "and—and Ma—Machine is thirty-six and Gunnar is fifty-eight—yes, that's right—and Maudey was my mother. She was my mother. She was ninety. But she didn't look it. She's dead. She didn't look it, did she? She took that stuff. She didn't look it."

"Baby," said Alyx, finding her voice, "look at me."

"Why?" said Iris in a whisper.

"Because," said Alyx, "I am going to tell you something horrible. Now look at me. You know what I look like. You've seen me in the daylight. I have lines in my face, the first lines, the ones that tell you for the first time that you're going to die. There's gray in my hair, just a little, just enough to see in a strong light, a little around my ears and one streak starting at my forehead. Do you remember it?"

Iris nodded solemnly.

"I am getting old," said Alyx, "and my skin is getting coarse and tough. I tire more easily. I am withering a little. It will go faster and faster from now on and soon I will die.

"Iris," she said with difficulty, "how old am I?"

"Fifty?" said Iris.

Alyx shook her head.

"Sixty?" said Iris hopefully.

Alyx shook her head again.

"Well, how old are you?" said Iris, a little impatiently.

"Twenty-six," said Alyx. Iris put her hands over her eyes.

"Twenty-six," said Alyx steadily. "Think of that, you

thirty-three-year-old adolescent! Twenty-six and dead at fifty. Dead! There's a whole world of people who live like that. We don't eat the way you do, we don't have whatever it is the doctors give you, we work like hell, we get sick, we lose arms or legs or eyes and nobody gives us new ones, we die in the plague, one-third of our babies die before they're a year old and one time out of five the mother dies, too, in giving them birth."

"But it's so long ago!" wailed little Iris.

"Oh no it's not," said Alyx. "It's *right now*. It's going on right now. I lived in it and I came here. It's in the next room. I was in that room and now I'm in this one. There are people still in that other room. They are living *now*. They are suffering *now*. And they always live and always suffer because *everything keeps on happening*. You can't say it's all over and done with because it isn't; it keeps going on. It all keeps going on. Shall I tell you about the plague? That's one nice thing. Shall I tell you about the fevers, the boils, the spasms, the fear, the burst blood vessels, the sores? Shall I tell you what's going on right now, right here, right in this place?"

"Y—yes! Yes! Yes!" cried Iris, her hands over her ears. Alyx caught the hands in her own, massaging them (for they were bare), slipping Iris's gloves back on and pressing the little tabs that kept them shut.

"Be quiet," she said, "and listen, for I am going to tell you about the Black Death."

And for the next half hour she did until Iris's eyes came back into focus and Iris began to breathe normally and at last Iris fell asleep.

Don't have nightmares, baby, said Alyx to herself, stroking one lock of silver hair that stuck out from under the girl's hood. *Don't have nightmares, thirty-three-year-old baby.* She did not know exactly what she herself felt. She bedded down in her own place, leaving all that for the next day, thinking first of her own children: the two put out to nurse, the third abandoned in the hills when she had run away from her husband at seventeen and (she thought) not to a Youth Core. She smiled in the dark. She wondered if Gunnar had known who was carrying on so. She wondered if he minded. She thought again of Iris, of Machine, of the comfort it was to hear human breathing around you at night, the real comfort.

I've got two of them, she thought, *and damn Gunnar anyway.*

She fell asleep.

The thirty-fifth day was the day they lost Raydos. They did not lose him to the cats, although they found big paw-prints around their camp the next morning and met one of the spotted animals at about noon, circling it carefully at a distance while it stood hissing and spitting on a rocky eminence, obviously unsure whether to come any closer or not. It was less than a meter high and had enormous padded paws: a little animal and a lot of irritation; Alyx dropped to the rear to watch it stalk them for the next three hours, keeping her crossbow ready and making abrupt movements from time to time to make it duck out of sight. Gunnar was up front, leading the way. Its persistence rather amused her at first but she supposed that it could do a lot of damage in spite of its size and was beginning to wonder whether she could risk a loud shout—or a shot into the rocks—to drive it off, when for no reason at all that she could see, the animal's tufted ears perked forward, it crouched down abruptly, gave a kind of hoarse, alarmed growl and bounded awkwardly away. The whole column in front of her had halted. She made her way to the front where Gunnar stood like a huge statue, his big arm pointing up straight into the sky, as visible as the Colossus of Rhodes.

"Look," he said, pleased, "a bird." She yanked at his arm, pulling him to the ground, shouting "Down, everyone!" and all of them fell on to their hands and knees, ducking their heads. The theory was that the white suits and white packs would blend into the snow as long as they kept their faces hidden, or that they would look like animals and that any reading of body heat would be disregarded as such. She wondered if there was any sense to it. She thought that it might be a bird. It occurred to her that distances were hard to judge in a cloudless sky. It also occurred to her that the birds she knew did not come straight down, and certainly not that fast, and that the snow-shoed cat had been running away from something snow-shoed cats did not like. So it might be just as well to occupy their ridiculous position on the ground until whatever it was satisfied its curiosity and went away, even though her knees and elbows hurt and she was getting the cramp, even though things were absolutely silent, even though nothing at all seemed to be happening . . .

"Well?" said Gunnar. There was a stir all along the line.

"Sssh," said Alyx. Nothing happened.

"We've been down on our knees," said Gunnar a bit testily, "for five minutes. I have been looking at my watch."

"All right, I'll take a look up," said Alyx, and leaning on one arm, she used her free hand to pull her hood as far over her face as possible. Slowly she tilted her head and looked.

"Tell us the color of its beak," said Gunnar.

There was a man hanging in the air forty meters above them. Forty meters up in the sky he sat on nothing, totally unsupported, wearing some kind of green suit with a harness around his waist. She could have sworn that he was grinning. He put out one bare hand and punched the air with his finger; then he came down with such speed that it seemed to Alyx as if he must crash; then he stopped just as abruptly, a meter above the snow and two in front of them. He grinned. Now that he was down she could see the faint outline of what he was traveling in: a transparent bubble, just big enough for one, a transparent shelf of a seat, a transparent panel fixed to the wall. The thing made a slight depression in the snow. She supposed that she could see it because it was not entirely clean. The stranger took out of his harness what even she could recognize as a weapon, all too obviously shaped for the human hand to do God knew what to the human body. He pushed at the wall in front of him and stepped out—swaggering.

"Well?" said Gunnar in a strained whisper.

"His beak," said Alyx distinctly, "is green and he's got a gun. Get up," and they all rocketed to their feet, quickly moving back; she could hear them scrambling behind her. The stranger pointed his weapon and favored them with a most unpleasant smile. He lounged against the side of his ship. It occurred to Alyx with a certain relief that she had known him before, that she had known him in two separate millennia and eight languages, and that he had been the same fool each time; she only hoped mightily that no one would get hurt. She hugged herself as if in fear, taking advantage of the position to take off her gloves and loosen the knives in her sleeves while Machine held his crossbow casually and clumsily in one hand. He was gaping at the stranger like an idiot. Gunnar had drawn himself up, half a head above all of them, again the colossus, his face pale and muscles working around his mouth.

"Well, well," said the stranger with heavy sarcasm, "break my———" (she did not understand this) "I'm just cruising around and what do I find? A bloody circus!"

Someone—probably a nun—was crying quietly in the back.

"And what's *that?*" said the stranger. "A dwarf? The Herculean Infant?" He laughed loudly. "Maybe I'll leave it alone. Maybe if it's female, I'll tuck it under my arm after I've ticked the rest of you and take it away with me for convenience. Some————!" and again a word Alyx did not understand. Out of the corner of her eye she saw Machine redden. The stranger was idly kicking the snow in front of him; then with his free hand he pointed negligently at Machine's crossbow. "What's that thing?" he said. Machine looked stupid.

"Hey come on, come on, don't waste my time," said the stranger. "What is it? I can tick you first, you know. Start telling."

"It's a d-d-directional f-f-inder," Machine stammered, blushing furiously.

"It's a what?" said the man suspiciously.

"It's t—to tell direction," Machine blurted out. "Only it doesn't work," he added stiffly.

"Give it here," said the stranger. Machine obligingly stepped forward, the crossbow hanging clumsily from his hand.

"*Stay back!*" cried the man, jerking up his gun. "*Don't come near me!*" Machine held out the crossbow, his jaw hanging.

"Stuff it," said the stranger, trying to sound cool, "I'll look at it after you're dead," and added, "Get in line, Civs," as if nothing at all had happened. *Ah yes,* thought Alyx. They moved slowly into line, Alyx throwing her arms around Machine as he stepped back, incidentally affording him the cover to pull back the bow's spring and giving herself the two seconds to say "Belly." She was going to try to get his gun hand. She got her balance as near perfect as she could while the stranger backed away from them to survey the whole line; she planned to throw from her knees and deflect his arm upward while he shot at the place she had been, and to this end she called out "Mister, what are you going to do with us?"

He walked back along the line, looking her up and down—mostly down, for he was as tall as the rest of them; possibly a woman as small as herself was a kind of expensive rarity. He said, "I'm not going to do anything to *you*."

"No," he said, "not to you; I'll leave you here and pick you up later, Infant. We can all use you." She looked innocent.

"After I tick these Ops," he went on, "after we get 'em melted—you're going to see it, Infant—then I'll wrap you up and come back for you later. Or maybe take a little now. We'll see.

"The question," he added, "is which of you I will tick first. The question is which of you feather-loving Ops I will turn to ashes first and I think, after mature judgment and a lot of decisions and maybe just turning it over in my head, I say I think—"

Gunnar threw himself at the man.

He did so just as Alyx flashed to her knees and turned into an instant blur, just as Machine whipped up the crossbow and let go the bolt, just as Gunnar should have stood still and prayed to whatever gods guard amateur explorers—just at this moment he flung himself forward at the stranger's feet. There was a flash of light and a high-pitched, horrible scream. Gunnar lay sprawled in the snow. The stranger, weapon dangling from one hand, bleeding in one small line from the belly where Machine's bolt had hit him, sat in the snow and stared at nothing. Then he bent over and slid onto his side. Alyx ran to the man and snatched the gun from his grasp but he was unmistakably dead; she pulled one of her knives out of his forearm where it had hit him—but high, much too high, damn the balance of the stupid things!—hardly even spoiling his aim—and the other from his neck, grimacing horribly and leaping aside to keep from getting drenched. The corpse fell over on its face. Then she turned to Gunnar.

Gunnar was getting up.

"Well, well," said Machine from between his teeth, "what—do—you—know!"

"How the devil could I tell you were going to do anything!" shouted Gunnar.

"Did you make that noise for effect," said Machine, "or was it merely fright?"

"Shut up, you!" cried Gunnar, his face pale.

"Did you wish to engage our sympathies?" said Machine, "or did you intend to confuse the enemy? Was it electronic noise? Is it designed to foul up radar? Does it contribute to the electromagnetic spectrum? Has it a pattern? Does it scan?"

Gunnar stepped forward, his big hands swinging. Machine raised the bow. Both men bent a little at the knees. Then in between them, pale and calm, stepped one of the nuns, looking first at one and then at the other until Gunnar turned his back and Machine—making a face—broke apart the crossbow and draped both parts over his shoulder.

"Someone is hurt," said the nun.

Gunnar turned back. "That's impossible!" he said. "Anyone in the way of that beam would be dead, not hurt."

"Someone," repeated the nun, "is hurt," and she walked back towards the little knot the others had formed in the snow, clustering about someone on the ground. Gunnar shouted, "It's not possible!"

"It's Raydos," said Machine quietly, somewhere next to Alyx. "It's not Iris. He just got the edge. The bastard had put it on diffuse. He's alive," and taking her by the elbow, he propelled her to the end of the line, where Raydos had been standing almost but not quite in profile, where the stranger had shot when his arm was knocked away and up from his aim on Gunnar, when he had already turned his weapon down on Gunnar because Gunnar was acting like a hero, and not tried to shoot Alyx, who could have dropped beneath the beam, twisted away and killed him before he could shoot again. Strike a man's arm up into the air and it follows a sweeping curve.

Right over Raydos's face.

And Raydos's eyes.

She refused to look at him after the first time. She pushed through the others to take a long look at the unconscious man's face where he lay, his arms thrown out, in the snow: the precise line where his face began, the

107

precise line where it ended, the fine, powdery, black char that had been carefully laid across the rest of it. Stirred by their breath, the black powder rose in fine spirals. Then she saw the fused circles of Raydos's eye lenses: black, shiny black, little puddles resting as if in a valley; they still gave out an intense heat. She heard Gunnar say nervously "Put—put snow on it," and she turned her back remarking, "Snow. And do what you have to do." She walked slowly over to the transparent bubble. In the distance she could see some kind of activity going on over Raydos, things being brought out of his pack, all sorts of conferring going on. She carefully kicked snow over the dead body. She reflected that Paradise must know them all very well, must know them intimately, in fact, to find the levers to open them one by one until none of them were left or only she was left or none of them were left. Maudey. She stood aside carefully as Gunnar and Machine carried up something that was lacking a face—or rather, his face had turned lumpy and white—and put him in the transparent bubble. That is, Gunnar put him in, getting half in with him for the thing would not hold more than the head and arms of another occupant. Gunnar was taping Raydos to the seat and the walls and working on the control board. Then he said, "I'll set the automatic location signal to turn itself off an hour after sundown; he did say he was cruising."

"So you know something," said Machine. Gunnar went on, his voice a little high:

"I can coordinate it for the Pole station."

"So you are worth something," said Machine.

"They won't shoot him down," said Gunnar quickly. "They would but I've set it for a distress call at the co-ordinate location. They'll try to trap him.

"That's not easy," he added, "but I think it'll work. It's a kind of paradox, but there's an override. I've slowed him down as much as I can without shutting him off altogether, he may last, and I've tried to put in some indication of where we are and where we're headed but it's not equipped for that; I can't send out a Standard call or *they'll* come and pick him up, I mean the others, of course, they must have this section pretty well under control or they wouldn't be sending loners around here. And of course the heat burst registered, but they'll think it's him; he did say—"

"Why don't you write it, you bastard?" said Machine.

"Write?" said Gunnar.

"Write it on a piece of paper," said Machine. "Do you know what paper is? He has it in his pack. That stuff he uses for drawing is paper. Write on it!"

"I don't have anything to write with," said Gunnar.

"You stupid bastard," said Machine slowly, turning Raydos's pack upside down so that everything fell out of it: pens, black stuff, packets of things taped together, food, a kind of hinged manuscript, all the medicine. "You stupid, electronic bastard," he said, ripping a sheet from the manuscript, "this is paper. And this" (holding it out) "is artist's charcoal. Take the charcoal and write on the paper. If you know how to write."

"That's unnecessary," said Gunnar, but he took the

writing materials, removed his gloves and wrote laboriously on the paper, his hands shaking a little. He did not seem to be used to writing.

"Now tape it to the wall," said Machine. "No, the inside wall. Thank you. Thank you for everything. Thank you for your heroism. Thank you for your stupidity. Thank you—"

"I'll kill you!" cried Gunnar. Alyx threw up her arm and cracked him under the chin. He gasped and stumbled back. She turned to Machine. "You too," she said, "you too. Now finish it." Gunnar climbed half inside the bubble again and commenced clumsily making some last adjustments on the bank of instruments that hung in the air. The sun was setting: a short day. She watched the snow turn ruddy, ruddy all around, the fingerprints and smears on the bubble gone in a general, faint glow as the light diffused and failed, the sun sank, the man inside—who looked dead—wobbled back and forth as Gunnar's weight changed the balance of the delicate little ship. It looked like an ornament almost, something to set on top of a spire, someone's pearl.

"Is he dead?" said Alyx. Machine shook his head. "Frozen," he said. "We all have it in the packs. Slows you down. He may last."

"His eyes?" said Alyx.

"Why, I didn't think you cared," said Machine, trying to make it light.

"*His eyes!*"

Machine shrugged a little uncomfortably. "Maybe

yes, maybe no," he said, "but" (here he laughed) "one would think you were in love with the man."

"I don't know him," said Alyx. "I never knew him."

"Then why all the fuss, Tiny?" he said.

"You don't have a word for it."

"The hell I don't!" said Machine somewhat brutally. "I have words for everything. So the man was what we call an artist. All right. He used color on flat. So what? He can use sound. He can use things you stick your fingers into and they give you a jolt. He can use wires. He can use textures. He can use pulse-beats. He can use things that climb over you while you close your eyes. He can use combinations of drugs. He can use direct brain stimulation. He can use hypnosis. He can use things you walk on barefoot for all I care. It's all respectable; if he gets stuck in a little backwater of his field, that's his business; he can get out of it."

"Put his sketches in with him," said Alyx.

"Why?" said Machine.

"Because you don't have a word for it," she said. He shrugged, a little sadly. He riffled the book that had come from Raydos's pack, tearing out about half of it, and passed the sheets in to Gunnar. They were taped to Raydos's feet.

"Hell, he can still do a lot of things," said Machine, trying to smile.

"Yes," said Alyx, "and you will come out of this paralyzed from the neck down." He stopped smiling.

"But you will do a lot of things," she said. "Yes, you will get out of it. You will lose your body and Gunnar

will lose his—his self-respect; he will make one more
ghastly mistake and then another and another and in the
end he will lose his soul at the very least and perhaps
his life."

"You know all this," said Machine.

"Of course," said Alyx, "of course I do. I know it all.
I know that Gavrily will do something generous and
brave and silly and because he never in his life has
learned how to do it, we will lose Gavrily. And then
Iris—no, Iris has had it already, I think, and of course
the Heavenly Twins will lose nothing because they have
nothing to lose. Maybe they will lose their religion or
drop their pills down a hole. And I—well, I—my profession, perhaps, or whatever loose junk I have lying
around, because this blasted place is too good, you see,
too easy; we don't meet animals, we don't meet paid
professional murderers, all we meet is our own stupidity. Over and over. It's a picnic. It's a damned picnic. And Iris will come through because she never lives
above her means. And a picnic is just her style."

"What will you lose?" said Machine, folding his arms
across his chest.

"I will lose you," she said unsteadily, "what do you
think of that?" He caught her in his arms, crushing the
breath out of her.

"I like it," he whispered sardonically. "I like it, Tiny,
because I am jealous. I am much too jealous. If I
thought you didn't like me, I'd kill myself and if I
thought you liked Iris more than me, I'd kill her. Do
you hear me?"

"Don't be an ass," she said. "Let me go."

"I'll never let you go. Never. I'll die. With you."

Gunnar backed ponderously out of the bubble. He closed the door, running his hands carefully over the place where the door joined the rest of the ship until the crack disappeared. He seemed satisfied with it then. He watched it, although nothing seemed to happen for a few minutes; then the bubble rose noiselessly off the snow, went up faster and faster into the evening sky as if sliding along a cable and disappeared into the afterglow. It was going north. Alyx tried to pull away but Machine held on to her, grinning at his rival as the latter turned around, absently dusting his hands together. Then Gunnar groped for his gloves, put them on, absently looking at the two, at the others who had shared the contents of Raydos's pack and were flattening the pack itself into a shape that could be carried in an empty food container. There was the corpse, the man everyone had forgotten. Gunnar looked at it impersonally. He looked at Iris, the nuns, Gavrily, the other two: only seven of them now. His gloved hands dusted themselves together. He looked at nothing.

"Well?" drawled Machine.

"I think we will travel a little now," said Gunnar; "I think we will travel by starlight." He repeated the phrase, as if it pleased him. "By starlight," he said, "yes."

"By snowlight?" said Machine, raising his eyebrows.

"That too," said Gunnar, looking at something in the distance, "yes—that too—"

"Gunnar!" said Alyx sharply. His gaze settled on her.

"I'm all right," he said quietly. "I don't care who you play with," and he plodded over to the others, bent over, very big.

"I shall take you tonight," said Machine between his teeth; "I shall take you right before the eyes of that man!"

She brought the point of her elbow up into his ribs hard enough to double him over; then she ran through the powdery snow to the front of the little line that had already formed. Gunnar was leading them. Her hands were icy. She took his arm—it was unresponsive, nothing but a heavy piece of meat—and said, controlling her breathing, for she did not want him to know that she had been running—"I believe it is getting warmer."

He said nothing.

"I mention this to you," Alyx went on, "because you are the only one of us who knows anything about weather. Or about machinery. We would be in a bad way without you."

He still said nothing.

"I am very grateful," she said, "for what you did with the ship. There is nobody here who knows a damn thing about that ship, you know. No one but you could have—" (she was about to say *saved Raydos's life*) "done anything with the control board. I am grateful. We are all grateful.

"Is it going to snow?" she added desperately, "is it going to snow?"

"Yes," said Gunnar. "I believe it is."

"Can you tell me why?" said she. "I know nothing

about it. I would appreciate it very much if you could tell me why."

"Because it is getting warmer."

"*Gunnar!*" she cried. "*Did you hear us?*"

Gunnar stopped walking. He turned to her slowly and slowly looked down at her, blankly, a little puzzled, frowning a little.

"I don't remember hearing anything," he said. Then he added sensibly, "That ship is a very good ship; it's insulated; you don't hear anything inside."

"Tell me about it," said Alyx, her voice almost failing, "and tell me why it's going to snow."

He told her, and she hung on his arm, pretending to listen, for hours.

They walked by starlight until a haze covered the stars; it got warmer, it got slippery. She tried to remember their destination by the stars. They stopped on Paradise's baby mountains, under the vast, ill-defined shadow of something going up, up, a slope going up until it melted into the gray sky, for the cloud cover shone a little, just as the snow shone a little, the light just enough to see by and not enough to see anything at all. When they lay down there was a pervasive feeling of falling to the left. Iris kept trying to clutch at the snow. Alyx told them to put their feet downhill and so they did, lying in a line and trying to hold each other's hands. Gunnar went off a little to one side, to watch—or rather to listen. Everything was indistinct. Five minutes after everyone had settled down—she could still hear their small readjustments, the moving about, the occasional whispering—she discerned someone squatting at her feet, his arms about his knees, balanced just so. She held out one arm and he pulled her to her feet, putting his arms around her: Machine's face, very close in the white darkness. "Over there," he said, jerking his head towards the place where Gunnar was, perhaps sitting, perhaps standing, a kind of blot against the gray sky.

"No," said Alyx.

"Why not?" said Machine in a low, mocking voice. "Do you think he doesn't know?"

She said nothing.

"Do you think there's anyone here who doesn't know?" Machine continued, a trifle brutally. "When you go off, you raise enough hell to wake the dead."

She nudged him lightly in the ribs, in the sore place, just enough to loosen his arms; and then she presented him with the handle of one of her knives, nudging him with that also, making him take step after step backwards, while he whispered angrily:

"What the hell!

"Stop it!

"What are you doing!

"What the devil!"

Then they were on the other side of the line of sleepers, several meters away.

"Here," she whispered, holding out the knife, "take it, take it. Finish him off. Cut off his head."

"I don't know what you're talking about!" snapped Machine.

"But not with me," she said; "oh, no!" and when he threw her down onto the snow and climbed on top of her, shaking her furiously, she only laughed, calling him a baby, teasing him, tickling him through his suit, murmuring mocking love-words, half in Greek, the better to infuriate him. He wound his arms around her and pulled, crushing her ribs, her fingers, smothering her with his weight, the knees of his long legs digging one into her shin and one into her thigh; there would be spectacular bruises tomorrow.

"Kill me," she whispered ecstatically. "Go on, kill me, kill me! Do what you want!" He let her go, lifting himself up on his hands, moving his weight off her. He stared down at her, the mask of a very angry young man. When she had got her breath back a little, she said:

"My God, you're strong!"

"Don't make fun of me," he said.

"But you are strong," she said breathlessly. "You're strong. You're enormous. I adore you."

"Like hell," said Machine shortly and began to get up. She flung both arms around him and held on.

"Do it again," she said, "do it again. Only please, please, more carefully!" He pulled away, making a face, then stayed where he was.

"If you're making fun of me—" he said.

She said nothing, only kissed his chin.

"I hate that man!" he burst out. "I hate his damned

117

'acceptable' oddities and his—his conventional heroism and his—the bloody amateur!

"He's spent his life being praised for individualism," he went on, "*his* individualism, good God! Big show. Make the Civs feel happy. Never two steps from trans and ports and flyers. Medicine. High-powered this. High-powered that. 'Ooooh, isn't he marvel! Isn't he brave! Let's get a tape and go shooting warts with Gunnar! Let's get a tape and go swimming undersea in Gunnar!' He records his own brain impulses, did you know that?"

"No," said Alyx.

"Yes," said Machine, "he records them and sells them. Gunnar's battle with the monsters. Gunnar's narrow escape. Gunnar's great adventure. All that heroism. That's what they want. That's why he's rich!"

"Well, they certainly wouldn't want the real thing," said Alyx softly, "now would they?"

He stared at her for a moment.

"No," he said more quietly, "I suppose they wouldn't."

"And I doubt," said Alyx, moving closer to him, "that Gunnar is recording anything just now; I think, my dear, that he's very close to the edge now."

"Let him fall in," said Machine.

"Are you rich?" said Alyx. Machine began to weep. He rolled to one side, half laughing, half sobbing.

"I!" he said, "I! Oh, that's a joke!"

"I don't have a damn thing," he said. "I knew there would be a flash here—*they* knew but they thought they could get away—so I came. To get lost. Spent everything. But you can't get lost, you know. You can't get lost anywhere any more, not even in a—a—you would call it a war, Agent."

"Funny war," said Alyx.

"Yes, very funny. A war in a tourist resort. I hope we don't make it. I hope I die here."

She slid her finger down the front of his suit. "I hope not," she said. "No," she said (walking both hands up and down his chest, beneath the long underwear, her little moist palms) "I certainly hope not."

"You're a single-minded woman," said Machine dryly.

She shook her head. She was thoughtfully making the tent of the night before. He helped her.

"Listen, love," she said, "I have no money, either, but I have something else; I am a Project. I think I have cost a lot of money. If we get through this, one of the things this Project will need to keep it happy so it can go on doing whatever it's supposed to do is you. So don't worry about that."

"And you think they'll let you," said Machine. It was a flat, sad statement.

"No," she said, "but nobody ever 'let me do anything in my life before and I never let that stop me." They were lying on their sides face to face now; she smiled up at him. "I am going to disappear into this damned suit if you don't pull me up," she said. He lifted her up a little under the arms and kissed her. His face looked as if something were hurting him.

"Well?" she said.

"The Machine," he said stiffly, "is—the Machine is fond of the Project."

"The Project loves the Machine," she said, "so—?"

"I can't," he said.

She put her arm around the back of his neck and rubbed her cheek against his. "We'll sleep," she said. They lay together for some time, a little uncomfortable because both were balanced on their sides, until he turned over on his back and she lay half on him and half off, her head butting into his armpit. She began to fall asleep, then accidentally moved so that his arm cut off her breathing, then snorted. She made a little, dissatisfied noise.

"What?" he said.

"Too hot," she said sleepily, "blasted underwear," so with difficulty she took it off—and he took off his—and they wormed it out of the top of the suits where the hoods tied together and chucked it into the snow. She was breathing into his neck. She had half fallen asleep again when all of a sudden she woke to a kind of earthquake: knees in a tangle, jouncing, bruising, some quiet, vehement swearing and a voice telling her for God's sake to wake up. Machine was trying to turn over. Finally he did.

"Aaaaaah—um," said Alyx, now on her back, yawning.

"Wake up!" he insisted, grabbing her by both hips.

"Yes, yes, I am," said Alyx. She opened her eyes. He seemed to be trembling all over and very upset; he was holding her too hard, also.

"What is it?" she whispered.

120

"This is not going to be a good one," said Machine, "do you know what I mean?"

"No," said Alyx. He swore.

"Listen," he said shakily, "I don't know what's the matter with me; I'm falling apart. I can't explain it, but it's going to be a bad one; you'll just have to wait through it."

"All right, all right," she said, "give me a minute," and she lay quietly, thinking, rubbing his hair—looked Oriental, like a brush now, growing into a peak on his forehead—began kissing various parts of his face, put her arms around his back, felt his hands on her hips (too hard; she thought *I'll be black and blue tomorrow*), concentrated on those hands, and then began to rub herself against him, over and over and over, until she was falling apart herself, dizzy, head swimming, completely out of control.

"God damn it, you're making it worse!" he shouted.

"Can't help it," said Alyx. "Got to—come on."

"It's not fair," he said, "not fair to you. Sorry."

"Forgiven," Alyx managed to say as he plunged in, as she diffused over the landscape—sixty leagues in each direction—and then turned into a drum, a Greek one, hourglass-shaped with the thumped in-and-out of both skins so extreme that they finally met in the middle, so that she then turned inside-out, upside-down and switched right-and-left sides, every cell, both hands, each lobe of her brain, all at once, while someone (anonymous) picked her up by the navel and shook her violently in all directions, remarking "If you don't make them cry, they won't live." She came to herself with the idea that Machine was digging up rocks. He was banging her on the head with his chin. Then after a while he stopped and she could feel him struggle back to self-possession; he took several deep, even breaths; he opened the suit hoods and pushed his face over her shoulder into the snow; then he opened one side of the little tent and let in a blast of cold air.

"Help!" said Alyx. He closed the suits. He leaned on his elbows. He said "I like you. I like you too much. I'm sorry." His face was wet to her touch: snow, tears or sweat. He said "I'm sorry, I'm sorry. We'll do it again."

"Oh no, no, no," she whispered weakly.

"Yes, don't worry," he said. "I'll control myself, it's not fair. No technique."

"If you use any more technique," she managed to get out, "there'll be nothing left of me in the morning but a pair of gloves and a small, damp spot."

"Don't lie," said Machine calmly.

She shook her head. She plucked at his arms, trying to bring his full weight down on her, but he remained propped on his elbows, regarding her face intently. Finally he said:

"Is that pleasure?"

"Is what?" whispered Alyx.

"Is it a pleasure," he said slowly, "or is it merely some detestable intrusion, some unbearable invasion, this being picked up and shaken, this being helpless and—and smashed and shattered into pieces when somebody lights a fuse at the bottom of one's brain!"

"It was pleasure for me," said Alyx softly.

"Was it the same for you?"

She nodded.

"I hate it," he said abruptly. "It was never like this before. Not like this. I hate it and I hate you."

She only nodded again. He watched her somberly.

"I think," he added finally, "that one doesn't like it or dislike it; one loves it. That is, something picked me up by the neck and pushed me into you. Ergo, I love you."

"I know," she said.

"It was not what I wanted."

"I know." She added, "It gets easier." He looked at her again; again she tried to pull him down. Then he remarked "We'll see," and smiled a little; he closed his eyes and smiled. He let his whole weight down on her carefully, saying, "You'll have to scramble out when I get too heavy, Tiny."

"Will."

"And tomorrow night," he added grimly, "I'll tell you the story of my life."

"Nice," she said, "yes, oh that will be . . . nice . . ." and she sank down deliciously into a sleep of feathers, into the swan's-down and duck's-down and peacock's-down that made up the snow of Paradise, into the sleep and snow of Paradise . . .

The next day Paradise threw hell at them. It was the

first real weather. It began with fat, heavy flakes just before dawn so that Gavrily (who had taken the dawn watch) was half buried himself and had to dig out some of the sleepers before he could rouse them; they were so used to the feeling of the stuff against their faces or leaking into their hoods and up their arms that they slept right through it. It turned colder as they ate breakfast, standing around and stamping and brushing themselves; then the snow got smaller and harder and then the first wind blasted around an outcropping of rock. It threw Alyx flat on her back. Gunnar said expressionlessly "You're smaller than we are." The others immediately huddled together. Goggles had not been packed with their equipment. They started out with the wind slamming them from side to side as if they had been toys, changing direction every few seconds and driving into their faces and down their necks stinging grains of rice. Gunnar insisted they were in a pass. They stumbled and fell more often than not, unable to see ten feet on either side, reaching in front of them, holding on to each other and sometimes falling onto hands and knees. Gunnar had faced away from the wind and was holding with both bare hands onto a map he had made from some of Raydos's things. He said "This is the pass." One of the nuns slipped and sprained her back. Gunnar was holding the map close to his eyes, moving it from side to side as if trying to puzzle something out. He said again:

"This is the pass. What are you waiting for?"

"What do you think, you flit!" snapped Iris. She was

on one side of the sister and Gavrily on the other, trying to haul the woman to her feet. Gunnar opened his mouth again. Before he could speak, Alyx was at him (clawing at the bottom of his jacket to keep from falling in the wind) and crushing the map into a ball in his hand. "All right, all right!" she shouted through the snow, "it's the pass. Machine, come on," and the three of them plodded ahead, feeling and scrambling over hidden rocks, up a slope they could not see, veiled in snow that whipped about and rammed them, edging on their hands and knees around what seemed like a wall.

Then the wind stopped and Machine disappeared at the same time. She could not see where he had gone for a moment; then the wind returned—at their backs—and blasted the snow clear for a moment, hurrying it off the rock wall in sheets and revealing what looked like a well in the rock and a great, flattened slide of snow near it. It looked as if something had been dragged across it. Then the snow swept back, leaving only a dark hole.

"Chimney!" said Gunnar. Alyx flung herself on the ground and began to inch towards the dark hole in the snow. "I can't see," she said. She went as close as she dared. Gunnar stood back at a little distance, bracing himself against the wall. She risked lifting one hand to wave him closer, but he did not move. "Gunnar!" she shouted. He began to move slowly towards her, hugging the wall; then he stopped where the wall appeared to stop, taking from inside his glove the crumpled map and examining it, bracing himself automatically as the wind rocked him back and forth, and tracing something on the map with one finger as if there were something that puzzled him.

"Gunnar," said Alyx, flattening herself against the ground, "Gunnar, this hole is too broad for me. I can't climb down it."

Gunnar did not move.

"Gunnar," said Alyx desperately, "you're a mountain climber. You're an expert. You can climb down."

He raised his eyes from the map and looked at her without interest.

"You can climb down it," continued Alyx, digging her fingers into the snow. "You can tie a rope to him and then you can climb up and we'll pull him up."

"Well, I don't think so," he said. He came a little closer, apparently not at all bothered by the wind, and peered into the hole; then he repeated in a tone of finality, "No, I don't think so."

"You've got to," said Alyx. He balled up the map again and put it back into his glove. He had turned and was beginning to plod back towards the place where they had left the others, bent halfway into the wind, when she shouted his name and he stopped. He came back and looked into the hole with his hands clasped behind his back; then he said:

"Well, I don't think I'll try that."

"He's dying," said Alyx.

"No, I think that's a little risky," Gunnar added reasonably. He continued to look into the hole. "I'll let you down," he said finally. "Is that all right?"

"Yes, that's all right," said Alyx, shutting her eyes. She considered kicking him or tripping him so that he'd fall in himself but he was keeping a very prudent distance from the edge, and besides, there was no telling where he would fall or how badly Machine was hurt. He might fall on Machine. She said, "That's fine, thanks." She rolled over and half sat up, slipping off her pack; clinging to it, she got out the length of rope they all carried and tied it under her arms. She was very clumsy in the wind; Gunnar watched her without offering to help, and when she was finished he took the free end and held it laxly in one hand. "Your weight won't be too much," he said.

"Gunnar," she said, "hold that thing right." He shook himself a little and took a better hold on the rope. Coming closer, he said "Wait a minute," rummaged in her pack and handed her a kind of bulb which she tucked into her sleeve. It looked like the medicine he had once shown her, the kind they had used on Raydos. He said "Put it in the crook of his arm and press it. A little at a time." She nodded, afraid to speak to him. She crawled toward the edge of the well where the snow had suddenly collapsed under Machine, and throwing her arms over the ground, let herself down into the dark. The rope held and Gunnar did not let go. She imagined that he would wait for her to shout and then throw down his own rope; she wrapped her arms around her head for the hole was too wide for her to brace herself and she spun slowly around—or rather, the walls did, hitting her now and then—until the chimney narrowed. She climbed

part of the way down, arms and legs wide as if crucified.
She had once seen an acrobat roll on a wheel that way.
The darkness seemed to lighten a little and she thought
she could see something light at the bottom, so she
shouted "Gunnar!" up the shaft. As she had expected,
a coil of rope came whispering down, settled about her
shoulders, slid off to one side and hung about her like a
necklace, the free end dangling down into the half-
dark.

But when she pulled at it, she found that the other
end was fastened under her own arms.

She did not think. She was careful about that. She
descended further, to where Machine lay wedged like
a piece of broken goods, his eyes shut, one arm bent at
an unnatural angle, his head covered with blood. She
could not get at his pack because it was under him. She
found a kind of half-shelf next to him that she could
stay on by bracing her feet against the opposite wall,
and sitting there, she took from her sleeve the bulb
Gunnar had given her. She could not get at either of
Machine's arms without moving him, for the other one
was twisted under him and jammed against the rock,
but she knew that a major blood vessel was in the crook
of the arm, so she pressed the nose of the bulb against
a vessel in his neck and squeezed the bulb twice. Nothing happened. She thought: *Gunnar has gone to get the
others.* She squeezed the medicine again and then was
afraid, because it might be too much; someone had said
"I've given Raydos all he can take"; so she put the thing
back in her sleeve. Her legs ached. She could just about

reach Machine. She took off a glove and put one hand in front of his mouth to satisfy herself that he was breathing, and then she tried feeling for a pulse in his throat and got something cold, possibly from the medicine bottle. But he had a pulse. His eyes remained closed. In her own pack was a time-telling device called a watch—she supposed vaguely that they called it that from the watches they had to keep at night, or perhaps they called it that for some other reason—but that was up top. She could not get to it. She began to put her weight first on one leg and then on the other, to rest a little, and then she found she could move closer to Machine, who still lay with his face upward, his eyes shut. He had fallen until the narrow part of the chimney stopped him. She was beginning to be able to see better and she touched his face with her bare hand; then she tried to feel about his head, where he was hurt, where the blood that came out increased ever so little, every moment, steadily black and black. The light was very dim. She felt gashes but nothing deep; she thought it must have been a blow or something internal in the body, so she put the medicine bulb to his neck again and squeezed it. Nothing happened. *They'll be back*, she thought. She looked at the bottle but could not see well enough to tell what was written on it so she put it back into her sleeve. It occurred to her then that they had never taught her to read, although they had taught her to speak. Lines came into her mind, *We are done for if we fall asleep*, something she must have heard; for she was growing numb and beginning to fall asleep, or not sleep exactly but some kind of retreat, and the dim, squirming walls around her began to close in and draw back, the way things do when one can barely see. She put both hands on Machine's face where the blood had begun to congeal in the cold, drew them over his face, talked to him steadily to keep herself awake, talked to him to wake him up. She thought *He has concussion,* the word coming from somewhere in that hypnotic hoard they had put into her head. She began to nod and woke with a jerk. She said softly "What's your name?" but Machine did not move. "No, tell me your name," she persisted gently, "tell me your name," drawing her hands over his face, unable to feel from the knees down, trying not to sink into sleep, passing her fingers through his hair while she nodded with sleep, talking to him, whispering against his cheek, feeling again and again for his hurts, trying to move her legs and coming close enough to him to see his face in the dim, dim light; to put her hands against his cheeks and speak to him in her own language, wondering why she should mind so much that he was dying, she who had had three children and other men past counting, wondering how there could be so much to these people and so little, so much and so little, like the coat of snow that made everything seem equal, both the up and the down, like the blowing snow that hid the most abysmal poverty and the precious things down under the earth. She jerked awake. Snow was sifting down on her shoulders and something snaky revolved in the air above her.

But Machine had stopped breathing some time before. She managed to wind her own rope loosely around her neck and climb the other by bracing herself against the side of the well: not as smoothly as she liked, for the rope wavered a little and tightened unsteadily while Alyx cursed and shouted up to them to mind their bloody business if they didn't want to get it in a few minutes. Gavrily pulled her up over the edge.

"Well?" he said. She was blinking. The four others were all on the rope. She smiled at them briefly, slapping her gloves one against the other. Her hands were rubbed raw. The wind, having done its job, had fallen, and the snow fell straight as silk sheets.

"Well?" said Gavrily again, anxiously, and she shook her head. She could see on the faces of all of them a strange expression, a kind of mixed look as if they did not know what to feel or show. Of course; they had not liked him. She jerked her head towards the pass. Gavrily looked as if he were about to say something, and Iris as if she were about to cry suddenly, but Alyx only shook her head again and started off behind Gunnar. She saw one of the nuns looking back fearfully at the hole. They walked for a while and then Alyx took Gunnar's arm, gently holding on to the unresponsive arm of the big, big man, her lips curling back over her teeth on one side, involuntarily, horribly. She said:

"Gunnar, you did well."

He said nothing.

"You ought to have lived in my country," she said. "Oh yes! you would have been a hero there."

She got in front of him, smiling, clasping her hands together, saying "You think I'm fooling, don't you?" Gunnar stopped.

"It was your job," he said expressionlessly.

"Well, of course," she said sweetly, "of course it was," and crossing her hands wrist to wrist as she had done a thousand times before, she suddenly bent them in and then flipped them wide, each hand holding a knife. She bent her knees slightly; he was two heads taller and twice as heavy, easily. He put one hand stupidly up to his head.

"You can't do this," he said.

"Oh, there's a risk," she said, "there's that, of course," and she began to turn him back towards the others as he automatically stepped away from her, turning him in a complete circle to within sight of the others, while his face grew frightened, more and more awake, until he finally cried out:

"Oh God, Agent, what will you do!"

She shifted a little on her feet.

"I'm not like you!" he said, "I can't help it, what do you expect of me?"

"He came and got us," said Iris, frightened.

"None of us," said Gunnar quickly, "can help the way we are brought up, Agent. You are a creature of your world, believe me, just as I am of mine; I can't help it; I wanted to be like you but I'm not, can I help that? I did what I could! What can a man do? What do you expect me to do? What could I do!"

"Nothing. It's not your job," said Alyx.

"I am ashamed," said Gunnar, stammering, "I am ashamed, Agent, I admit I did the wrong thing. I should have gone down, yes, I should have—put those things away, for God's sake!—forgive me, please, hate me but forgive me; I am what I am, I am only what I am! For Heaven's sake! For God's sake!"

"Defend yourself," said Alyx, and when he did not —for it did not seem to occur to him that this was possible—she slashed the fabric of his suit with her left-hand knife and with the right she drove Trans-Temp's synthetic steel up to the hilt between Gunnar's ribs. It did not kill him; he staggered back a few steps, holding his chest. She tripped him onto his back and then cut his suit open while the madman did not even move, all this in an instant, and when he tried to rise she slashed him through the belly and then—lest the others intrude —pulled back his head by the pale hair and cut his throat from ear to ear. She did not spring back from the blood but stood in it, her face strained in the same involuntary grimace as before, the cords standing out on her neck. Iris grabbed her arm and pulled her away.

"He came and got us," whispered Iris, terrified, "he did, he did, really."

"He took his time," said Gavrily slowly. The five of them stood watching Gunnar, who lay in a red lake. The giant was dead. Alyx watched him until Iris turned her around; she followed obediently for a few steps, then stopped and knelt and wiped her hands in the snow. Then putting on her gloves, she took handfuls of snow and rubbed them over her suit, up and down, up and down. She cleaned herself carefully and automatically, like a cat. Then she put the knives away and silently followed the four others up the pass, floundering and slipping through the still-falling snow, hunched a little, her fists clenched. At dusk they found a shallow cave at the bottom of a long slope, not a rock cave but soft rock and frozen soil. Gavrily said they were over the pass. They sat as far back against the cave wall as they could, watching the snow fall across the opening and glancing now and again at Alyx. She was feeling a kind of pressure at the back of her neck, something insistent like a forgotten thought, but she could not remember what it was; then she took the medicine bulb out of her sleeve and began playing with it, tossing it up and down in her hand. That was what she had been trying to remember. Finally Iris giggled nervously and said:

"What are you doing with that?"

"Put it in your pack," said Alyx, and she held it out to the girl.

"*My* pack?" said Iris, astonished. "Why?"

"We may need it," said Alyx.

"Oh Lord," said Iris uncomfortably, "we've still got enough to eat, haven't we?"

"Eat?" said Alyx.

"Sure," said Iris, "that's lecithin. From synthetic milk," and then she clapped both hands across her mouth as Alyx leapt to her feet and threw the thing out into the falling snow. It seemed to Alyx that she had suddenly walked into an enormous snake, or a thing like one of the things that cleaned up houses in civilized countries: something long, strong and elastic that winds around you and is everywhere the same, everywhere equally strong so that there is no relief from it, no shifting it or getting away from it. She could not bear it. She did not think of Machine but only walked up and down for a few minutes, trying to change her position so that there would be a few minutes when it would not hurt; then she thought of a funnel and something at the bottom of it; and then finally she saw him. Wedged in like broken goods. She thought *Wedged in like broken goods*. She put her hands over her eyes. The same face. *The same face*. Iris had gotten up in alarm and put one hand on Alyx's shoulder; Alyx managed to whisper "Iris!"

"Yes? Yes?" said Iris anxiously.

"Get those damned women," said Alyx hoarsely for now he was all over the cave, pale, eyes shut, on every wall, irretrievably lost, a smashed machine with a broken arm at the bottom of a rock chimney somewhere. It was intolerable. For a moment she thought that she was bleeding, that her arms and legs were cut away. Then that disappeared. She put out her hands to touch his face, to stay awake, to wake him up, again and again and again, and then this would not stop but went on and on in a kind of round dance that she could not control, over and over in complete silence with the cold of the rock-chimney and the dim light and the smell of the place, with Machine still dead, no matter what she did, lying on top of his pack and not speaking, wedged into the rock like a broken toy with one leg dangling. It kept happening. She thought *I never lost anything before*. She cried out in her own language.

When the sister came with the pill-box to comfort her, Alyx wrenched the box out of the woman's hand, swallowed three of the things, shoved the box up her own sleeve—above the knife-harness—and waited for death.

But the only thing that happened was that the nuns got frightened and retreated to the other end of the cave.

And Alyx fell asleep almost instantly.

She woke up all at once, standing, like a board hit with a hoe; Paradise—which had been stable—turned over once and settled itself. This was interesting but not novel. She looked outside the cave, forgot what she had seen, walked over to the nuns and pulled one of them up by the hair, which was very amusing; she did it to the other, too, and then when the noise they made had waked up Iris and Gavrily, she said "Damn it, Gavrily, you better be careful, this place has it in for me."

He only blinked at her. She pulled him outside by one arm and whispered it fiercely into his ear, pulling him down and standing on her toes to do so, but he remained silent. She pushed him away. She looked at his frightened face and said contemptuously "Oh, you! you can't hear," and dropped her pack into the snow; then when somebody put it on her back she dropped it again; only the third time she lost interest. They put it on again and she forgot about it. By then they were all up and facing out onto the plains, a flat land covered with hard snow, a little dirty, like pulverized ice, and a brown haze over the sky so that the sun showed through it in an unpleasant smear: she wanted to look at it and would not go anywhere until someone pushed her. It was not an attractive landscape and it was not an unattractive one; it was fascinating. Behind her Gavrily began to sing:

> "When I woke up, my darling dear,
>   When I woke up and found you near,
>   I thought you were an awful cutie
>   And you will always be my sweetie."

She turned around and shouted at him. Someone gave a shocked gasp. They prodded her again. She found Iris at her elbow, quite unexpectedly pushing her along, and began to explain that her feet were doing that part of the work. She was very civil. Then she added:

"You see, I am not like you; I am not doing anything idiotic or lying in the snow making faces. I haven't lost my head and I'm going on in a perfectly rational manner; I can still talk and I can still think and I wish to the devil you would stop working my elbow like a pump; it is very annoying, besides being entirely unnecessary. You are not a nice girl."

"I don't know that language," said Iris helplessly, "what are you saying?"

"Well, you're young," said Alyx serenely, "after all."

At midday they let her look at the sky.

She lay down flat in the snow and watched it as the others ate, through a pair of binoculars she had gotten from someone's pack, concentrating on the detail work and spinning the little wheel in the middle until Iris grabbed her hands and hoisted her to her feet. This made her cross and she bit Iris in the arm, getting a mouthful of insulated suit. She seriously considered that Iris had played a trick on her. She looked for the binoculars but they were not around; she lagged after Iris with her gloves dangling from her wrists and her bare fingers making circles around her eyes; she tried to tell Iris to look at that over there, which is what that which it is, and then a terrible suspicion flashed into her mind in one sentence:

You are going out of your mind.

Immediately she ran to Iris, tugging at Iris's arm, holding her hand, crying out "Iris, Iris, I'm not going out of my mind, am I? Am I going out of my mind? Am I?" and Iris said "No, you're not; come on, *please*," (crying a little) and the voice of one of the Hellish Duo sounded, like an infernal wind instrument creeping along the bottom of the snow, in a mean, meaching, nasty tone, just like the nasty blur in the brown sky, an altogether unpleasant, exceptionable and disgusting tone:

"She's coming out of it."

"How can I come on if I'm coming out?" demanded Alyx, going stiff all over with rage.

"Oh, please!" said Iris.

"How," repeated Alyx in a fury, "can I come on if I'm coming out? How? I'd like you to explain that"—her voice rising shrilly—"that—conundrum, that impossibility, that flat perversion of the laws of nature; it is absolutely and utterly impossible and you are nothing but an excuse, an evasion, a cheap substitute for a human being and a little tin whore!"

Iris turned away.

"But how can I!" exploded Alyx. "How can I be on and out? How can I? It's ridiculous!"

Iris began to cry. Alyx folded her arms around herself and sunk her head on her chest; then she went over to Iris and patted Iris with her mittens; she would have given up even the sky if it made Iris unhappy. She said reassuringly "There, there."

"Just come on, please," said Iris. Subdued, Alyx followed her. A great while after, when she had put down the other foot, Alyx said "You understand, don't you?" She took Iris's arm, companionably.

"It's only the pills," said Iris, "that's all."

"I never take them," said Alyx.

"Of course not," said Iris.

Curiously Alyx said, "Why are you shaking?"

They walked on.

Towards evening, long after the immense day had sunk and even the diffused light died out so that the bottom of the plain was nothing but a black pit, though even then the snow-luminescence glowed about them vaguely, not enough to see by *but enough* (Alyx thought) *to make you take a chance and break your neck*—she realized that they had been handing her about from one to the other all day. She supposed it was the pills. They came and went in waves of unreason, oddly detached from herself; she dozed between them as she walked, not thinking of suggesting to the others that they stop, and when they did stop she merely sat down on the snow, put her arms around her knees and stared off into the darkness. Eventually the light from the snow failed. She felt for the box in her sleeve and laughed a little; someone near her stirred and whispered "What? What?" and then yawned. The breathing fell again into its soft, regular rhythm. Alyx laughed again, dreamily, then felt something in back of her, then turned around to look for it, then found nothing. It was in back of her again. She yawned. The darkness was becoming uncomfortable. She fought the desire to sleep. She felt about and nudged the person nearest her, who immediately sat up—to judge from the sound—and gave out a kind of "Ha!" like a bellows. Alyx laughed.

"Wha'—huh!" said Gavrily.

"Look," she said sensibly, "about these pills. What do they do to you?"

"Muh," said Gavrily.

"Well, how many can I take?" said Alyx, amused.

"Take what?"

"Take pills," said Alyx.

"What? Don't take any," he said. He sounded a little more awake.

"How many," said Alyx patiently, "can I take without hurting myself?"

"None," said Gavrily. "Bad for the liver. Meta—metabol—give 'em back."

"You won't get them," said Alyx. "Don't try. How many can I take without making a nuisance of myself?"

"Huh?" said Gavrily.

"How many?" repeated Alyx. "One?"

"No, no," said Gavrily stupidly, "none," and he muttered something else, turned over in the dark and apparently fell asleep. She heard him snore; then it was turned off into a strangled, explosive snort and he breathed like a human being. Alyx sat peering keenly into the dark, feeling them come closer and closer and smiling to herself. When the world was about to touch her—and she would not stand for that—she took out her little box. She broke a pill and swallowed half. She came to the surface nonetheless, as one does when breaking the surface of water, blinded, chilled, shocked by the emptiness of air; the snow solidified under her, her suit began to take shape and grate like iron, the sleepers next to her emerged piecemeal out of the fog, grotesquely in separate limbs, in disconnected sounds, there were flashes of realization, whole moments of absolute reality. It simply would not do. She grinned nervously and hugged her knees. She blinked into the darkness as if her eyes were dazzled; she held on to her knees as a swimmer holds on to the piles of a jetty with his fingertips, she who had never been drunk in her life because it impaired the reason. She stuffed the box back up her sleeve. Eventually something happened—she shook her head as if to get rid of a fly or a nervous tic—the water rose. It closed over her head. She yawned. With her mouth wide open, water inside, water outside, she slid down, and down, and down, singing like a mermaid: *I care for nobody, no, not I.* She slept.

And nobody cares for me.

The false dawn came over the flats, bringing nothing with it.

She sat and considered her sins.

That they were vast was undeniably true, a mental land as flat and bare as a world-sized table, and yet with here and there those disturbing dips and slides: concave surfaces that somehow remained flat, hills that slid the other way, like the squares on a chessboard which bend and produce nausea. Such places exist.

Her sins were terrible. She was staring at a pink marble bathtub, full of water, a bathtub in which she had once bathed in the palace of Knossos on Crete, and which now hung on the ceiling overhead. The water was slipping. She was going to be drowned. The ocean stuck to the sky, heaving. In her youth she had walked town streets and city streets, stolen things, been immensely popular; it had all come to nothing. Nothing had come out of nothing. She did not regret a single life lost. In the snow appeared a chessboard and on the chessboard figures, and these figures one by one slid down into

squares in the board and disappeared. The squares puckered and became flat. She put her fingers into them but
they would not take her, which was natural enough in a
woman who had not even loved her own children. You
could not trust anyone in those times. The electromagnetic spectrum was increasing. Slowly the plains filled
with air, as a pool with water; an enormous racket went
on below the cliff that was the edge of the earth; and
finally the sun threw up one hand to grasp the cliff,
climbed, clung, rose, mounted and sailed brilliantly white
and clear into a brilliant sky.

It said to her, in the voice of Iris: "You are frozen
through and through. You are a detestable woman."

She fell back against the snow, dead.

When the dawn came, bringing a false truce, Alyx was
sitting up with her arms clasped about her knees and
watching the others wake up. She was again, as before,
delicately iced over, on the line between reason and unreason. She thought she would keep it that way. She
ate with the others, saying nothing, doing nothing,
watching the murky haze in the sky and the spreading
thumbprint in it that was the sun. The landscape was
geometric and very pleasing. In the middle of the morning they passed a boulder someone or something had put
out on the waste: to one side of it was a patch of
crushed snow and brown moss showing through. Later
in the day the world became more natural, though no
less pleasant, and they stopped to eat once more, sitting

in the middle of the plain that spread out to nowhere in particular. Iris was leaning over and eating out of one hand, utterly beautiful as were all the others, the six or seven or eight of them, all very beautiful and the scenery too, all of which Alyx explained, and that at very great length.

"What do you mean!" cried Iris suddenly. "What do you mean you're going to go along without us, what do you mean by that!"

"Huh?" said Alyx.

"And don't call me names," said Iris, trembling visibly. "I've had enough," and she went off and sat by somebody else. *What have you had enough of?* thought Alyx curiously, but she followed her anyway, to see that she came to no harm. Iris was sitting by one of the nuns. Her face was half turned away and there was a perceptible shadow on it. The nun was saying "Well, I told you." The shadow on Iris's face seemed to grow into a skin disease, something puckered or blistered like the lichens on a rock, a very interesting purple shadow; then it contracted into a small patch on her face and looked as if it were about to go out, but finally it turned into something.

Iris had a black eye.

"Where'd you get that?" said Alyx, with interest.

Iris put her hand over her eye.

"Well, where'd you get it?" said Alyx. "Who gave it to you? Did you fall against a rock?

"I think you're making it up," she added frankly, but the words did not come out quite right. The black eye wavered as if it were going to turn into a skin disease again. "Well?" demanded Alyx. "How'd you get it out here in the middle of the desert? Huh? How did you? Come on!"

"You gave it to me," said Iris.

"Oh, she won't understand anything!" exclaimed one of the nuns contemptuously. Alyx sat down in the snow and tucked her feet under her. She put her arms around herself. Iris was turning away again, nursing the puffy flesh around her bloodshot eye: it was a purple bruise beginning to turn yellow and a remarkable sight, the focus of the entire plain, which had begun to wheel slowly and majestically around it. However, it looked more like a black eye every moment.

"*Me?*" Alyx said finally.

"In your sleep," answered one of the nuns. "You are certainly a practiced woman. I believe you are a bad woman. We have all tried to take the pills away from you and the only issue of it is that Iris has a black eye and Gavrily a sprained wrist. Myself, I wash my hands of it.

"Of course," she added with some satisfaction, "it is too late now. Much too late. You have been eating them all along. You can't stop now; you would die, you know. Metabolic balances."

"What, in one night!" said Alyx.

"No," said the other. "Five."

"I think we are running out of food," said Iris. "We had better go on."

"Come on," she added, getting up.

They went on.

She took command two days later when she had become more habituated to the stuff, and although someone followed them constantly (but out of sight) there
were no more hallucinations and her decisions were—
on the whole—sensible. She thought the whole thing
was a grand joke. When the food disappeared from out
of the bottomless bags, she turned them inside out and
licked the dust off them, and the others did the same;
when she bent down, supporting herself on one arm,
and looked over the brown sky for aircraft, the others
did the same; and when she held up two fingers
against one eye to take the visual diameter of the bleary
sun and then moved the two fingers three times to
one side—using her other hand as a marker—to find
out their way, so did they, though they did not know
why. There was no moss, no food, hardly any light, and
bad pains in the stomach. Snow held them up for a day
when the sun went out altogether. They sat together
and did not talk. The next day the sky lifted a little and
they went on, still not talking. When the middle of the
day came and they had rested a while, they refused to
get up; so she had to pummel them and kick them to
their feet. She said she saw a thing up ahead that was
probably the Pole station; she said they had bad eyes
and bad ears and bad minds and could not expect to see
it. They went on for the rest of the day and the next

morning had to be kicked and cuffed again until they got up, and so they walked slowly on, leaving always the same footprints in the thin snow, a line of footprints behind exactly matching the fresh line in front, added one by one, like a line of stitching. Iris said there was a hobby machine that did that with only a single foot, faster than the eye could follow, over and over again, depositing now a rose, now a face, again a lily, a dragon, a tower, a shield . . .

On the fifty-seventh day they reached the Pole station. It sprawled over five acres of strangely irregular ground: cut-stone blocks in heaps, stone paths that led nowhere, stone walls that enclosed nothing, a ruined city, entirely roofless. Through their binoculars nothing looked taller than any of them. Nothing was moving. They stood staring at it but could make no sense of it. One of the nuns flopped down in the snow. Gavrily said:

"Someone ought to let them know we're here."

"They know," said Alyx.

"They don't know," he said.

"They know," said Alyx. She was looking through the binoculars. She had her feet planted wide apart in the snow and was fiddling with the focus knob, trying to find something in the ruins. Around her the women lay like big dolls. She knew it was the Pole because of the position of the sun; she knew it was not a city and had never been a city but something the lieutenant had long ago called a giant aerial code and she knew that if someone does not come out to greet you, you do not run to greet him. She said "Stay here," and hung the binoculars around her neck.

"No, Agent," said Gavrily. He was swaying a little on his feet.

"Stay here," she repeated, tucking the binoculars inside her suit, and dropping to her knees, she began to crawl forward. Gavrily, smiling, walked past her towards the giant anagram laid out on the snow; smiling, he turned and waved, saying something she could not catch; and resolutely marching forward—because he could talk to people best, she supposed, although he was stumbling a little and his face was gray—he kept on walking in the direction of the Pole station, over the flat plain, until his head was blown off.

It was done silently and bloodlessly, in a flash of light. Gavrily threw up both arms, stood still, and toppled over. Behind her Alyx heard someone gasp repeatedly, in a fit of hiccoughs. Silence.

"Iris, give me your pack," said Alyx.

"Oh no, no, no, no, no, no, no, no," said Iris.

"I want to go away," said someone else, tiredly.

Alyx had to kick them to get the packs off them; then she had to push Iris's face into the snow until the girl stopped grabbing at her; she dragged all four packs over the snow like sleds, and stopping a few feet from Gavrily's body, she dumped all four onto the ground and pulled Gavrily back by the feet. *Marker,* she thought. Cursing automatically, she wrenched the packs open and lobbed a few bottles at the town at random. They vanished in a glitter two meters from the ground. She thought for a moment and then rapidly assembled a crossbow; bolts fired from it met the same fate; the crossbow itself, carefully lifted into the air, flared at the tip and the whole thing became so hot that she had to drop it. Her gloves were charred. Wrapping bandages from one of the packs around the bow, she lifted it again, this time ten paces to one side; again the tip vanished; ten paces to the other side and the same thing happened; crawling forward with her sunglasses on, she held it up in front of her and watched the zone of disappearance move slowly down to the grip. She tried it with another, twenty paces to the left. Twenty paces to the right. Her palms were blistered, the gloves burned off. The thing got closer and closer to the ground; there would be no crawling under it. She retreated to Gavrily's body and found Iris behind it, holding on to one of the packs to keep herself steady, whispering "What is it, what is it, what is it?"

"It's a fence," said Alyx, thrusting her stinging hands into the snow, "and whoever's running it doesn't have the sense to turn it off."

"Oh no, it's a machine," whispered Iris, laying her head against the pack, "it's a machine, it's no use, there's nobody there."

"If there were nobody there," said Alyx, "I do not think they would need a fence—Iris!" and she began shaking the girl, who seemed to be falling asleep.

"Doesn't know anything," said Iris, barely audible. "Idiots. Doesn't care."

"Iris!" shouted Alyx, slapping her, "Iris!"

"Only numbers," said Iris, and passed out. Alyx pulled her over by one shoulder and rubbed snow on her face. She fed her snow and put her forefingers under the girl's ears, pressing hard into the glands under them. The pain brought the girl around; "Only numbers," she said again.

"Iris," said Alyx, "give me some numbers."

"I.D.," said Iris, "on my back. Microscopic."

"Iris," said Alyx slowly and distinctly, "I cannot read. You must count something out for me. You must count it out while I show those bastards that there is somebody out here. Otherwise we will never get in. We are not supposed to be recognized and we won't be. We are camouflaged. You must give me some numbers."

"Don't know any," said Iris. Alyx propped her up against what was left of one of the packs. She dozed off. Alyx brought her out of it again and the girl began to cry, tears going effortlessly down her cheeks, busily one after the other. Then she said "In the Youth Core we had a number."

"Yes?" said Alyx.

"It was the number of our Core and it meant the Jolly Pippin," said Iris weakly. "It went like this—" and she recited it.

"I don't know what those words mean," said Alyx; "you must show me," and holding up Iris's hand, she watched while the girl slowly stuck up fingers: five seven seven, five two, seven five five six. Leaving Iris with her head propped against the pack, Alyx wound everything she could around the base of one of the crossbows, and lifting it upwards slowly spelled out five seven seven, five two, seven five five six, until everything was gone, when she wound another pack around another bow, leaving the first in the snow to cool, and again spelled out the number over and over until she could not move either hand, both hurt so abominably, and Iris had passed out for the second time.

Then something glittered in the middle of the Pole station and figures in snowsuits came running through the heaps of stone and the incomplete stone walls. Alyx thought dryly *It's about time.* She turned her head and saw the nuns tottering towards her, she thought suddenly *God, how thin!* and feeling perfectly well, she got up to wave the nuns on, to urge them to greet the real human beings, the actual living people who had finally come out in response to Iris's Jolly Pippin. A phrase she had heard sometime during the trip came to her mind: The Old School Yell. She stepped forward smartly and gestured to one of the men, but as he came closer—two others were picking up Iris, she saw, and still others racing towards the nuns—she realized that he had no face, or none to speak of, really, a rather amusing travesty or approximation, that he was, in fact, a machine like the workers she had seen in the sheds when they had first set out on their picnic. Someone had told her then "They're androids. Don't nod." She continued to wave. She turned around for a last look at

Paradise and there, only a few meters away, as large as life, stood Machine with his arms crossed over his chest. She said to him "What's a machine?" but he did not answer. With an air of finality, with the simplicity and severity of a dying god, he pulled over his blue eyes the goggled lenses and snout of another species, rejecting her, rejecting all of them; and tuned in to station Nothing (twenty-four hours a day every day, someone had said) he turned and began to walk away, fading as he walked, walking as he went away, listening to Trivia between the earth and the air until he walked himself right into a cloud, into nothing, into the blue, blue sky.

Ah, but I feel fine! thought Alyx, and walking forward, smiling as Gavrily had done, she saw under the hood of her android the face of a real man. She collapsed immediately.

Three weeks later Alyx was saying goodbye to Iris on the Moondrom on Old Earth, a vast idiot dome full of mist and show-lights, with people of all sorts rising and falling on streams of smoke. Iris was going the cheap way to the Moon for a conventional weekend with a strange young man. She was fashionably dressed all in silver, for that was the color that month: silver eyes, silvered eyelids, a cut-out glassene dress with a matching cloak, and her silver luggage and coiffure, both vaguely spherical, bobbing half a meter in the air behind their owner. It would have been less unnerving if the hair had been attached to Iris's head; as it was, Alyx could not keep her eyes off it.

Moreover, Iris was having hysterics for the seventh time in the middle of the Moondrom because her old friend who had gone through so much with her, and had taught her to shoot, and had saved her life, would not tell her anything—anything—anything!

"Can I help it if you refuse to believe me?" said Alyx.

"Oh, you think I'll tell *him!*" snapped Iris scornfully, referring to her escort whom neither of them had yet met. She was searching behind her in the air for something that was apparently supposed to come out of her luggage, but didn't. Then they sat down, on nothing.

"Listen, baby," said Alyx, "just listen. For the thirty-third time, Trans-Temp is not the Great Trans-Temporal Cadre of Heroes and Heroines and don't shake your head at me because it *isn't*. It's a study complex for archaeologists, that's all it is, and they fish around blindfold in the past, love, just as you would with a bent pin; though they're very careful where and when they fish because they have an unholy horror of even chipping the bottom off a canoe. They think the world will blow up or something. They stay thirty feet above the top of the sea and twenty feet below it and outside city limits and so on and so on, just about everything you can think of. And they can't even let through anything that's alive. Only one day they were fishing in the Bay of Tyre a good forty feet down and they just happened to receive twenty-odd cubic meters of sea-water complete with a small, rather inept Greek thief who had just pinched an expensive chess set from the Prince of Tyre, who between ourselves is no gentleman. They tell me I was attached to a rope attached to knots attached to a rather large boulder with all of us considerably more dead than alive, just dead enough, in fact, to come through at all, and just alive enough to be salvageable. That is, I was. They also tell me that this is one chance in several billion billion so there is only one of me, my dear, only one, and there never will be any more, prehistoric or heroic or unheroic or otherwise, and if you would only please, please oblige your escort by telling—"

"They'll send you back!" said Iris, clasping her hands with wonderful intensity.

"They can't," said Alyx.

"They'll cut you up and study you!"

"They won't."

"They'll shut you up in a cage and make you teach them things!"

"They tried," said Alyx. "The Army—"

Here Iris jumped up, her mouth open, her face clouding over. She was fingering something behind her ear.

"I have to go," she said absently. She smiled a little sadly. "That's a very good story," she said.

"Iris—" began Alyx, getting up.

"I'll send you something," said Iris hastily. "I'll send you a piece of the Moon; see if I don't."

"The historical sites," said Alyx. She was about to say something more, something light, but at that moment

Iris—snatching frantically in the air behind her for what-ever it was that had not come out the first time and showed no signs of doing so the second—burst into pas-sionate tears.

"How will you manage?" she cried, "oh, how will you, you're seven years younger than I am, you're just a *baby!*" and weeping in a swirl of silver cloak, and hair, and luggage, in a storm of violently crackling sparks that turned gold and silver and ran off the both of them like water, little Iris swooped down, threw her arms around her littler friend, wept some more, and immediately afterward rose rapidly into the air, waving goodbye like mad. Halfway up to the foggy roof she produced what she had apparently been trying to get from her luggage all along: a small silver flag, a jaunty square with which she blew her nose and then proceeded to wave goodbye again, smiling brilliantly. It was a handkerchief.

Send me a piece of the Moon, said Alyx silently, *send me something I can keep,* and turning away she started out between the walls of the Moondrom, which are walls that one cannot see, through the cave that looks like an enormous sea of fog; and if you forget that it was made for civilized beings, it begins to look, once you have lost your way, like an endless cave, an end-less fog, through which you will wander forever.

But of course she found her way out, finally.

At the exit—and it was the right exit, the one with billowing smoke that shone ten thousand colors from the lights in the floor and gave you, as you crossed it, the faint, unpleasant sensation of being turned slowly upside down, there where ladies' cloaks billowed and transparent clothing seemed to dissolve in streams of fire—

Stood Machine. Her heart stopped for a moment, automatically. The fifth or sixth time that day, she estimated.

"God save you, mister," she said.

He did not move.

"They tell me you'll be gone in a few weeks," she said. "I'll be sorry."

He said nothing.

"They also tell me," she went on, "that I am going to teach my special and peculiar skills in a special and peculiar little school, for they seem to think our pilgrimage a success, despite its being full of their own inexcusable blunders, and they also seem to think that my special and peculiar skills are detachable from my special and peculiar attitudes. Like Iris's hair. I think they will find they are wrong."

He began to dissolve.

"Raydos is blind," she said, "stone blind, did you know that? Some kind of immune reaction; when you ask them, they pull a long face and say that medicine can't be expected to do everything. A foolproof world and full of fools. And then they tape wires on my head and ask me how it feels to be away from home; and they shake their heads when I tell them that I am not away from home; and then they laugh a little—just a little—when I tell them that I have never had a home.

"And then," she said, "I tell them that you are dead."

He disappeared.

"We'll give them a run for their money," she said. "Oh yes we will! By God we will! Eh, love?" and she stepped through the smoke, which now contained nothing except the faint, unpleasant sensation of being turned slowly upside down.

Iris may turn out to be surprisingly accurate, she thought, *about the Great Trans-Temporal Cadre of Heroes and Heroines.*

Even if the only thing trans-temporal about them is their attitudes. The attitudes that are not detachable from my special and peculiar skills.

If I have anything to say about it.

WINNER OF
THE HUGO AWARD
AND THE
NEBULA AWARD
FOR BEST
SCIENCE FICTION
NOVEL OF
THE YEAR

Babel 17 Delany $1.25

Big Time Leiber   95c

City Simak $1.25

Dragon Masters Vance   95c

Dream Master Zelazny $1.25

Dune Herbert $1.50

Einstein Intersection Delany   95c

Four For Tomorrow Zelazny $1.25

Left Hand of Darkness LeGuin $1.50

Rite of Passage Panshin $1.25

Swords and Deviltry   Leiber $1.25

This Immortal Zelazny   ·$1.25

Available wherever paperbacks are sold or use this coupon.

7E

FRITZ LEIBER

062190	The Big Time	95c
791525	Swords Against Death	$1.25
791723	Swords and Deviltry	$1.25
791624	Swords Against Wizardry $1.25	
791822	Swords in the Mist	$1.25
792226	The Swords of Lankhmar $1.25	
951467	You're All Alone	95c

6F

URSULA K. LEGUIN

.... 107029 City of Illusion — $1.25
.... 478024 Left Hand of Darkness — $1.50
.... 669531 Planet of Exile — $1.25
.... 732925 Roncannon's World — $1.25
.... 900779 A Wizard of Earthsea — $1.25

Available wherever paperbacks are sold or use this coupon.

---

ace books, (Dept. MM) Box 576, Times Square Station
New York, N.Y. 10036

Please send me titles checked above.

I enclose $............... Add 20¢ handling fee per copy.

Name ....

Address ....

City...................... State............. Zip........

33E

Decadent future meets survival past
Alyx is past —
Alyx falls in love w/a machine
machine dies,